A Quest for Love and Glory!

Mandricardo and Callipygia: he a stalwart knight from Tartary and friend and comrade to Kesrick of Dragonrouge; she an Amazonian of uncommon beauty and ability. Together they happily roved Terra Magica until a misplaced wish ruthlessly bespelled them apart.

And seeking each other through all the known, lesser known, and unknown lands, Mandricardo and Callipygia embarked on an incredible adventure which would see them pitted against the Evil Magicians' and Wicked Enchanters' Guild, caught up in the titanic clash between a mighty Roc and a mountainous genie, and confronted with all the fabulous monsters and menaces of this most fantastical of fantasy realms!

MANDRICARDO

Author's Note

Terra Magica is an alternate world, as close to our own as are two pages in a book; so close that our most sensitive artists, dreamers, and poets glimpse something of its woods and fields, its tall cities and splendid heroes; thus, the history of Terra Magica becomes the substance of our epics and sagas, our myths and legends, fantasies and fairy tales.

This is the third novel I have written about Terra Magica. The first two, both published by DAW Books, were *Kesrick* (1982) and *Dragonrouge* (1984); they were both drawn from a distinguished volume of history (history in Terra Magica, anyway) called *The True and Veritable History of the Knight of Dragonrouge*.

The present volume, *Mandricardo*, is drawn from the sequel to the *True and Veritable History*, called the *Chronicle Narrative of the Deeds of Mandricardo*, a history no less distinguished than its predecessor.

Each volume of this sequence can be read separately and independently of each other. In fact, that's part of the fun!

———Lin Carter

Montclair, New Jersey

MANDRICARDO

New Adventures in Terra Magica

LIN CARTER

DAW BOOKS, INC.
DONALD A. WOLLHEIM, PUBLISHER

1633 Broadway, New York, NY 10019

First Printing, January 1987

1 2 3 4 5 6 7 8 9

PRINTED IN THE U.S.A.

This one is for Avram Davidson,
old friend, good man,
grand writer.

Contents

BOOK FOUR
Akhdar the Green

BOOK FIVE
Ithuriel

BOOK ONE

The Troll's Ring

1

Any Port in a Storm

It had started to snow quite soon after sunrise and by now the snow had clogged the trail, almost hiding it, and the going had become difficult. The man and the woman were well-mounted, but their horses (as well as the plump, frisky little mule who trotted obediently behind them, loaded with their luggage) were finding their footing slippery and uncertain. The snow was coming down quite heavily now, in thick, wet, fat, white flakes that always seemed to fly directly into their eyes, blinding them, or into their noses, making them sneeze. And it was piling up in slushy drifts that would probably have reminded the travelers of scoops of vanilla ice cream, except that vanilla ice cream had not been invented yet here in Terra Magica, the world next door to our own.

The man was a Tartar, dark and swarthy, tall and long-legged, and a knight, as you could have guessed from his flashing armor. He had a hooked nose, long drooping black moustachios, large very dark liquid eyes,

11

and he wore a spiked helmet. There were lion-skins draped about his brawny shoulders, the skins of lions he had hunted and slain himself, of course. His name was Sir Mandricardo, and he was the son of King Agricane of Tartary.

His steed was a magnificent coal-black charger named Bayardetto, which means "Little Bayard," and a handsome animal he was, as brave as a mastiff and every bit as faithful. Mandricardo had become very attached to the noble warhorse, for they had shared many adventures together, and on only *one* of these had Bayardetto displayed anything less than staunch courageousness. (That one time was when a giant the size of a small mountain had bent over and plucked a couple of Mandricardo's friends out of their saddles and swooped them up into the air . . . and Mandricardo thought it quite understandable for his horse to have acted *just a little nervous* on this occasion.)

By the side of the Tartar knight . . . well, no: *behind* him, actually, since the trail was so narrow they had to ride single file . . . pranced a fine red mare in whose saddle rode a young woman of abundant, more-than-ample charms. Her name was Princess Callipygia, and she was one of the seventeen daughters of the Queen of the Amazons and not only Mandricardo's girl-friend, but also his fiancée. She didn't wear much in the way of clothes: just some bits and pieces of armor, greaves and buskins, a gorget, gauntlets, girdle, a mail-skirt, and such like; also a cloak trimmed with fur. Amazons, as a rule, don't wear many clothes. I'm not sure exactly why.

The two had been houseguests at Dragonrouge, an old and stately home which belonged to their dear friends Sir Kesrick and his newly-wed bride, the Princess Arimaspia of Scythia. At the conclusion of their adventures together, Mandricardo and Callipygia had accom-

panied the Knight of Dragonrouge and his betrothed to
the ancestral home of Kesrick's fathers; they had stayed
for the wedding, of course, and for about two weeks
after the nuptials. Now it was time that they arranged
their own wedding, they thought; and thus had ridden
forth from the gates of Dragonrouge and, with the
blithe nonchalance of a hero and heroine in a chivalric
romance (which, of course, they actually *were*—and if
you doubt it, just keep reading), were perfectly prepared to ride horseback the entire width of the world
from the Frankish kingdom in the West to the famous
Kingdom of Tartary in the East, which is just before
you get to Cathay and a little bit north of Prester John's
Empire.

These countries exist only in Terra Magica, you understand; you will not find them on your maps of Terra
Cognita, the Lands We Know.

Your historian regrets having to admit that Mandricardo
was being a pain in the neck. He was even getting on
Callipygia's nerves a little, despite the fact that she
loved him dearly. Even being loved can't keep you
from getting on someone's nerves, it seems, and
Mandricardo had been grumbling and complaining for
hours now, ever since it had started to snow. Apparently it seldom snowed in Tartary, for the tall young
knight was not accustomed to putting up with the several discomforts associated with that climatic condition.

He complained that the snow was melting on his
helmet and dripping off, running in an icy trickle right
down the back of his neck, underneath his armor.

He complained that the flakes were blowing directly
into his eyes and blinding him, so that he couldn't see
where he was going.

He complained that if this sort of thing kept on much
longer, his armor would begin to get rusty and the

leather of his finely-tooled saddle would get moldy, and he would probably catch a cold in the head.

They were plodding along a narrow trail that wound between high hills crowned with thick dark woods, and the land was rising and getting rocky. There were cliffs up ahead, as far as Callipygia could tell, peering in between the snowflakes. It occurred to the Amazon girl that perhaps they could find shelter and build a fire.

"Cave or something, what?" murmured Mandricardo, a bit indistinctly, because his teeth were chattering. The snow had soaked his long droopy moustachios and then they had frozen, making it chilly for his upper lip.

"We may as well take a look," suggested Callipygia, guiding her red mare into the bushes beside the trail. She led the way through trees that loomed up, wet black shafts behind the veils of falling whiteness. With a dispirited shrug, Mandricardo guided his charger after her. Wet branches slapped him all over, sending a shower of half-melting snow down the back of his neck. A thicker branch caught his helmet a sound blow, tilting it rakishly over one eye.

"Oh, I say, dash it all!" he grumbled. But his companion was too far ahead to hear his words, luckily, for he was, as I have said, beginning to try her patience a little.

At length they emerged from the forest into a small clearing where the brisk wind was driving the snow wetly against gaunt cliffs. In those cliffs a black opening yawned. Callipygia prodded him in the ribs with a happy grin.

"There, by my halidom! What did I say? A cave—!" she cried. The Tartar knight eyed it dubiously, blinking the snowflakes out of his eyes.

"I say, Cally," he complained, "dash it all, but the place looks like one of those Troll caves dear old Kesrick was sayin' we might find up hereabouts. . . ."

The Amazon squared her shoulders and snatched out her sword, blue eyes snapping zestfully.

"Troll or no Troll," the girl said staunchly, "it's any port in a storm. Come *on!*"

Troll or no Troll, it became obvious as they approached that *somebody* made the cave his home, for it had a door: a strong, thick slab of stained wood, bound with heavy bolts of brass, standing ajar. Firelight flickered within—a very inviting sight, if you happen to be standing knee-deep in wet mushy snow, which they were, having dismounted. Leading their horses by the bridle, with the little mule following behind, they ventured as far as the cave's mouth, or door, as I should say. Peering within, they saw stalagmites hanging down from the smoke-blackened ceiling above (or do I mean stalactites?) and the walls of rough rock were hung with odds and ends of weaponry: axes, broadswords, spears and the like, all very, very old and every single one of them made of bronze.

"Why bronze, what?" muttered Mandricardo curiously.

"Shush! Because the one thing Trolls fear most is Cold Steel," whispered Callipygia, brandishing her naked blade, which caught the firelight and flashed like a mirror in the sun.

A frightened squeal from directly behind them nearly stampeded their horses. The two whirled about, to see—

"Oh, I say," faltered Mandricardo, "it really *is* a Troll's cave. And here's the bally old Troll!"

And so it was, for while neither of the two had ever laid eyes on a Troll before, suchlike creatures not being indigenous to Tartary or to Amazonia either, well, as the author of the *Chronicle Narrative of the Deeds of Mandricardo of Tartary* puts it in a clever phrase, "when once you see a Troll, there is no mistaking it for anything else." And such was the case precisely, for there it was—hairy as a thicket and huge as a hill—weak little pink eyes blinking fearfully on either side of its enormous proboscis of a nose, crowned with cow-horns, cow-tail dragging in the snow behind.

The monstrous creature had evidently been roaming the woods gathering fallen branches for its fire, for it held an armload of wet bare boughs, which it let fall at one glimpse of the deadly sheen and shimmer of Cold Steel.

Then, with a guttural croak, the Troll turned and waddled away, splayed feet and bowed legs working, disappearing in the dark woods.

They looked at each other, a wordless glance. Then the Amazon girl put away her glittering sword.

"I told you Trolls did not like the look of Cold Steel," said Callipygia, looking satisfied.

"Rah-*ther!*" said Mandricardo admiringly. "Chased the beggar off without a blow exchanged! Capital! Capital!"

They went in. The cavern was large and high-roofed; a huge fire burned briskly on the hearth, painting orange light and inky shadows over the rugged walls. Crude stools and a three-legged table were all of the furnishings; a heap of foul-smelling hides served the former occupant as a bed. The floor of the cave was littered with garbage, composed mostly of *bones*. The bones had been gnawed—you could see the tusk-marks! —then split lengthwise so as to suck out the marrow; Mandricardo and Callipygia fastidiously averted their eyes from the sight and pretended not to notice that some of the bones were *of human origin*.

Cupboards and rough shelves had been built along one wall. Callipygia eyed them speculatively, wondering if there was anything to eat therein, and if so, what Trolls happened to like to eat, when they were not

eating Meat. She rummaged therein, finding rags and a
few battered pots and pans (of brass or copper), a broken belt, some pieces of tough leather, and an ivory
needle as big as a dirk.

Mandricardo closed the door against the wintry blasts
and led Bayardetto over in front of the fire. Finding a
heap of rags, he began to rub down his charger, not
even bothering to take off his saddle first, because the
poor horse was soaking wet with snow.

"Just look at *this!*" the Amazon girl exclaimed, holding up a heavy bronze armlet she had just found in the
cupboard. It shone in the ruddy firelight and she marveled at the strange crooked characters carved about
the circle of bronze; they were letters in no language
known to Callipygia. Delighted with her discovery, she
tried the ring on: it fitted snugly about her biceps; she
twisted and turned it about, seeking the best angle to
display it, and as she did so, Mandricardo was complaining in his whining way.

"Ah? Very nice, I'm sure . . . I say! Dash it all, poor
Bayardetto; just *look* at the old fellow. Soaked to the
skin, he is, and shivering in all this bally snow—s-s—!"
And he threw back his head and sneezed tremendously.
"Now, you see, these Frankish winters—now I'm catching a cold in the head, I could feel it coming on, don't
you know . . . oh, I *do* wish we were somewhere warm
and dry—!"

Turning and twisting the bronze armlet on her upper
arm, trying to see which way it looked best on her,
Callipygia snapped at him. She was, by now, quite fed
up with her lover's unmanly complaining, so she re-
torted, "Well, I wish you *were!*"

Then her jaw dropped. Her eyes popped. She swayed
like a sapling in a tornado, turning the color of milk.

*For Mandricardo—and his noble charger—had just
vanished.*

For a moment, there, it looked very much as if Callipygia were about to faint dead away, like the heroine of some Victorian novel. However, the seventeen daughters of the Queen of the Amazons happen to be made of sterner stuff than are the heroines of Victorian novels, and the brawny girl soon recovered her composure.

She began to search the dark recesses of the Troll's cave, discovering many Nasty Things in the farthest corners where it was good and dark, but not finding a trace of the Tartar knight or his great black charger. The two had snapped out of existence the very instant she had voiced her wish that Mandricardo could have his wish and be somewhere warm and dry.

She had also been twisting and turning that bronze ring on her arm. Odd coincidence, but surely it meant nothing.

It did not at that time occur to Callipygia that if the bronze ring was big enough to fit around her upper arm, it was probably the right size to fit on one of the Troll's thick fingers.

Just like a Wishing ring. . . .

2

Consequences of Making a Wish

It proved quite an upsetting experience, as Mandricardo later remarked on more than one occasion: one moment he was soaked to the skin and shivering in the cold drafts of a Troll's drafty cave . . . then, in an eye-blink, he was ankle-deep in parched desert sands (a nice reddish saffron color) and staggering under the stunning weight of a furnace-like sun, blazing at the zenith of a cloudless sky. It is no wonder that Mandricardo gave voice to a startled yelp—followed by *a manly oath*—and that his horse shied and whinnied.

The Tartar knight stared around him incredulously. Hummocks of dust-dry desert sand undulated away in every direction, baked in the oven of noon. Something very like a range of miniature mountains marched from east to west (or was it north to south?—it was hard to tell); these last were too regular to be the work of Nature and had to be man-made. Their sides were sheathed in glistening limestone; stiff, throned figures

19

of solid gold, or what *appeared* to be solid gold, stood at the summit of each.

Mandricardo blinked at them. It took him only a dazed moment or two, or perhaps three, to recognize them, for they were every bit as famous in his world as they are in our own, except that in Terra Magica they happen to be in very much better repair.

"I *say*," he marveled. "Ruddy Pyramids, by Jove! But what are the bally things doing here in the middle of Frankland . . . and whatever happened to all that dratted *snow?*"*

The Tartar knight did not at once perceive that he had been magically transported a couple of thousands of miles East and South of where he had been an instant earlier. That's the trouble with traveling on a Wish; it happens so fast you don't realize at once that it has happened at all.

By now steam was rising from the lion-skins wrapped about Sir Mandricardo's shoulders and from his cloak, which was nearly dry, and from Bayardetto's sleek black hide. The desiccated desert air sucked every molecule of moisture from the outsides of both of them, and in a twinkling, too. Quite thawed, even comfortably warm at last, it was not very long before Mandricardo became uncomfortably hot. The sun was broiling and his steel armor was heating up. Perspiration went trickling down

---

*A reader of either Kesrick or of Dragonrouge, I forget which, wrote to ask me why Mandricardo, who is a Tartar, talks like one of the Knights of the Round Table (perhaps Sir Grummore Grummursum in The Sword in the Stone?). It's a perfectly legitimate question and perhaps I should have anticipated that some reader would ask it. Even far away in Tartary, as a boy Mandricardo read the histories of the Knights of the Round Table, which are histories in his world just as they are legends in our own, and so admired them that he grew up earnestly wishing to be a noble and knight like his heroes and have chivalric adventures. I suppose he imitated their speech automatically, and that that's where he picked up all those "by my halidom!" and "varlets" and other outmoded tags of speech.

the back of his neck, which was already reddening
from the scorching solar rays, and down his ribs.

In no time, he was as uncomfortably hot as he had
been uncomfortably cold and damp. Sometimes, there
is *no pleasing* a person, and Mandricardo was that kind
of person, at times. To be fair, in all that armor, he did
rather feel like a roast in the oven.

If only he could find some cool shade . . . but where?
There was none, not even over by those Pyramids, for
the sun stood directly at noon and not *a square inch* of
shade could the Tartar see. He vaulted into Bayardetto's
saddle, and from that vantage could just perceive an
oasis or something in the distance. Nodding palms with
fronds like splinters of emerald encircled a calm pool
like an oval of amethyst.

"Oh, I say, *that's* the ticket, what? Tally-ho!" sang Sir
Mandricardo, and they went cantering off toward the
oasis, or whatever it was.*

Desert sands are not quite the sort of thing for which
the hooves of horses were designed; it's solid, well-
packed turf for them. However, plodding along through
knee-deep sand is no harder than plodding along through
knee-deep snow had been, and it was all in a day's work
to Bayardetto.

Before long they had reached the shade of the palms,
and it was as blissfully cool as the Tartar knight had
guessed it would be. He dismounted and led his steed
to the margin of the calm pool, and they both knelt in
the rushes and drank thirstily. Then Mandricardo removed bit, bridle, and saddle and permitted his charger to wander about, cropping the sweet grass which
grew between the palms, while he scouted about for
something to eat. All of their provisions had been packed
away in the saddle-bags on the mule—and where was

*It was an oasis, but Mandricardo didn't know the word, apparently.

the mule now? For that matter, where was Callipygia, and what had happened to separate them?

"Magic, by gad!" snorted Mandricardo, scowling fiercely. "That dashed Troll—the varlet had some magic or other, and used it against us, just because we chased him out of his filthy old cave." The *sheer unfairness* of it all—well, words failed him!

An hour later found Mandricardo in a much better mood, and cured of those pangs of hunger which earlier had assailed his middle. Now he was comfortably seated cross-legged on a gorgeous carpet in the cool shade of a nodding palm, nibbling on olives, dates, wedges of fragrant cheese, salted almonds, ripe figs, the remnants of a broiled fowl sopping with spiced gravy, and sipping frozen sherbet from a small silver cup.

His host sat opposite him upon a similar rug. He was tall and lean, with coffee-colored skin, a thrusting beak of a hooked nose, and superb silver moustachios. He wore flowing robes, riding boots, and a striped head-dress of starched linen. He was the Sheikh Abdoul Achmed al-Abziz, and he had never before met a Tartar and was enchanted at the opportunity to do so.

This courteous and chivalric gentleman, a merchant whose caravan regularly used this oasis and others, urged more luncheon on his stalwart and swarthy guest. Mandricardo was nothing loath; plodding along mile after mile through all that filthy snow had given him a ravenous appetite.

"Pray satisfy my curiosity, Sir Mandricardo, as to what fair wind of happenstance brings you to this sunny land, so far from your own wind-scoured and wintry steppes?" inquired al-Abziz.

"Dashed if I can tell you that, old boy," confessed Mandricardo cheerfully, around another steaming mouthful of delicious fowl. "Don't understand it meself, you

know. Magic . . . that's the word for it. *Magic!*" he
hissed mysteriously. Then he told the old Sheikh about
the Troll's cave and the nice fire and so on, up to the
moment he had vanished from the cave and popped
into existence amidst the Trackless Sands.

Ah, doubtless that explained everything, the old Sheikh
nodded wisely. He was well acquainted with magic,
although not himself a magician, of course; still and all,
his maternal great-uncle, one Alcahazar by name, had
been quite a distinguished magician in his day. And
without further ado, as the sky turned to tangerine
touched with delicate wisps of gold, al-Abziz related to
his guest the surprising adventure of the Five Magicians . . . a narrative which, while of unsurpassed ex-
cellence, is much too lengthy to be quoted here, and,
as well, is not relevant to our story.

The small fire had dwindled to pulsing coals before
the merchant had finished his account of the adventure
of his maternal great-uncle, and by this time his Nubian
slaves were setting up two silken pavilions, one for
their master and one for his chance-met guest; other
servants had already fed and watered the camels and
were bedding these disagreeable beasts down for the
night.

The sky had become a remarkable turquoise by now,
dimming to sapphire above, where a full moon floated
like the globe of some enormous pearl. Mandricardo
and his host bade each other a polite good night and
retired to their slumbers.

With dawn, the Tartar knight rose from his bed in the
silken tent, rinsed his hands in rose water from Schiraz,
was shaved by the Sheikh's expert barber, and breakfasted off ripe oranges, seed-cakes, slices of spiced mut-
ton, and small porcelain cups of intensely hot, utterly
black, horribly sweet coffee.

Overnight, al-Abziz's slaves had cleaned and polished Mandricardo's armor, burnishing away every last speck or fleck of rust the snows of Frankland may have inflicted. As the caravan-master saw to the loading and mounting of the camels, the knight sought out his steed, who had been beautifully groomed, sumptuously fed and watered, and was as frisky as a colt.

Leaping into the saddle, Mandricardo reflected that if you must go about the wide world having adventures and fighting ogres and witches and things, it certainly makes it more comfy if you have a bunch of slaves along to shave you, cook for you, and tend to your bodily comforts.

They left the little oasis an hour past dawn and entered upon the last leg of their journey to the City of the Caliph which lay hard by. Bayardetto (who was not designed for deserts as the camels were) found the soft, cinnamon-colored sand tough going, but the warhorse plodded grimly on as Mandricardo, lounging in the saddle, chatted animatedly with his courtly host, who rode a camel.

"I say, al-Abziz, those are the famous Pyramids, what? Heard quite a bit about them, you know."

"They are indeed, good sir," replied the Sheikh. "They were built ages ago, some say by the ancient Kings of this land, while others argue that they were raised by the celebrated Soliman Djinn-ben-Djinn, mightiest of all the pre-Adamite Sultans."

"Ah, um," replied Sir Mandricardo.

Warming to his subject, the Sheikh continued: "There are more than eighty pyramids in all in our land, but these to our right are the first and most famous to be erected. The greatest is named 'Horizon of Cheops' and was built to house the remains of the first King of the Fourth Dynasty. The second pyramid is known as 'Great is Chephren,' and the third rejoices in the appellation of 'Divine is Mycerinius'; you will notice that is is the smallest of the three?"

"Ah, er," was Sir Mandricardo's response.

"We are close enough to the pyramid of Mycerinius for you to see the Guardian Idol which protects it from intruders. You will notice that the Idol is built of black and white onyx, with fierce sparkling jeweled eyes, that it sits enthroned and is armed with a spear of black stone. Ancient magicians cast powerful enchantments upon these Idols which guard the mightier pyramids; were you or I to approach more closely, the Guardian would rise from its throne of stone and menace us with its stone spear, which is longer than a weaver's beam and very much heavier."

"I say," breathed Mandricardo, his own eyes sparkling fiercely. He loved to hear about magic and magicians. Then he noticed a very much smaller pyramid all but drowned in the shadow of "Divine is Mycerinius." "Whatever is that very small one over there to the side? Tomb of one of the old King's wives, what?"

The dignified old merchant sniffed; his austere features frosted over with disapproval.

"Sad to say, such is not the case, by Mahoum!" said al-Abziz. "I very much fear that miniature pyramid was built to house the mortal remains of a notorious courtesan, one Rhodopis, and the labor of its construction was paid for, sayeth tradition, by the ill-gotten gains of that lady of ill-repute."

"You don't say?" marveled Mandricardo, measuring the small pyramid from base to apex. Although the smallest of the group, it was still of most respectable size, and must have cost a modest fortune in limestone, at least, not to mention granite. He opened his lips to inquire more interestedly into the life and times of this celebrated *femme de nuit*, but al-Abziz hastily changed the subject from one of ladies of loose morality, to the

famous Sphinx, which contains a secret burial chamber
wherein are held the bones of King Harmäis.

Having rested and refreshed themselves, the Sheikh
ordered his Nubians to strike the tent, pack the goods
and mount the camels. He was pleased to invite Sir
Mandricardo to accompany his caravan to the nearest
city, which stood not far off, to which invitation
Mandricardo gladly gave acceptance.

The camels, laden with bales of trade-goods, led the
way over the undulating dunes of cinnamon-colored
sand. Erelong the city whereof the friendly Sheikh had
spoken arose upon the horizon. And as the camel caravan drew nearer to its gates, Mandricardo could clearly
see the yellow mosques and green coppery domes of
the desert metropolis, and its black cypresses, and the
fronts of its marble palaces, and shining pillars, and
lofty carven arches that spanned half-circles of the hot
gray sky.

"By Jove," marveled Mandricardo, eyes sparkling with
excitement. They rode on, entering the city through a
vast portcullis gate.

3

Callipygia Presses On

When Callipygia had uttered her thoughtless wish and Mandricardo and his steed had snapped out of existence, the Amazon girl was, as you or I might well be, *quite overcome*. She dashed about the cave wildly, calling her lover's name in helpless tones which edged upon hysteria; a bit later, getting a grip on herself and keeping in mind that Amazons are certainly not given to fits of the vapors, she searched the cave from stem to stern, as you might say, finding absolutely nothing that assisted her toward a solution of her problem.

There were no trapdoors down through which the Tartar knight might conceivably have fallen, and no sliding panels in the walls (which, anyway, were solid rock), so the only answer to the mystery also began with the same letter, and that was *magic*.

During their adventures the length and breadth of Terra Magica, the Tartar and the Amazon had encountered many a villain, some with magic powers. In this regard, a witch named Mother Gothel and an enchanter

27

called Zazamanc sprang easily to mind. While either or
both had very sound and credible reasons for wishing to
cause Mandricardo and his lady-love discomforture, that
either had been the author of the present misfortune
was difficult to believe. That is, Mother Gothel had
earlier melted away when she had been caught by
surprise in a sudden rainstorm (water melts witches, as
you certainly ought to know), while the Egyptian sorcerer had been transformed to a marble statue when
one of his sorcerous spells had rebounded from Kesrick's
magic blade, Dastagerd, the Sword of Undoings.

And to tell the truth, Callipygia couldn't think of
anyone else in Terra Magica who might wish them ill.
Except for the Troll, of course . . . the poor ungainly
creature had doubtless been looking forward to a pleasant night in its snug and comfy cave, basking in the
warmth of a roaring fire while outside a stormy, snowy
night howled and blizzarded, if there *is* such a word,
and I am not altogether certain that there is. It had
been out in the dark woods replenishing the fuel supply
by picking up fallen branches when they had surprised
it, and right now, the Troll was probably huddled mourn-
fully, snuffling to itself and shuddering in the cold,
wishing them a thousand miles away and itself back in
the nice warm cave.

Did Trolls have magical powers? The Amazon girl bit
her underlip vexedly: the trouble was, she knew remarkably little about Trolls. There were no such creatures on Amazonia, unless you cared to count ogres,
who resembled them in certain features. She decided
after a bit that probably, when it came to magical
powers, Trolls were very much like men and women:
some had magic and some did not.

She wondered (if it was the Troll who was behind
Mandricardo's disappearance) why it had only struck at
the Tartar knight, without having a go at her. She also

wondered if, during the night, it might not attempt to break down the door and get in. The door was sound and solid enough, and it was locked and bolted, but she hauled some large and cumbersome articles of furniture against it, just to feel a bit safer.

As there was nothing to be done about Mandricardo's vanishing until daylight, Callipygia very sensibly put the problem out of her mind and made herself some supper. There wasn't much left in the saddlebags, and all she could find to eat in the Troll's cave was a very dry and rather huge wedge of cheese and half a barrel full of late apples, but she carved off a few slices of cheese and gnawed on the fruit and made the best of things.

She had to break up some of the Troll's furniture to feed the fire, but there was more than enough to last her through the night. Having eaten her meal and removed her armor, the Amazon princess stretched out before the fire under her blankets, placed her weapons close to hand, and went to sleep.

Sometime during the night the blizzard stopped and the next morning when Callipygia peeked out the door, she saw the forest was up to its knees in fresh-fallen snow which looked delightfully soft and fluffy. But then snow always looks nicer when you peer at it out of a warm house, or even a cozy cave, than it does when you are trying wearily to trudge through the nasty clinging stuff.

Over her meager breakfast of bread and cheese and a couple of the Troll's apples, Callipygia tried to figure out what to do.

"Either Mandricardo has been destroyed, or transformed into something else, or transported somewhere," the Amazon girl said to herself thoughtfully. "If he has been destroyed, well, that's that, and there is nothing I can do to help him unless mayhap to avenge his cruel fate . . . except that I have no idea who did the dastardly deed, unless it was that hulking great Troll."

She scratched her jaw meditatively. "And if he has only been transformed into something else, well, I will need the help of a friendly magician," she muttered beneath her breath. "I am a little short of friendly magicians right now. If I were back home, yes; of course; it would be no problem. But the only ones I know in these parts are old Atlantes and Dame Pirouetta. . . ."

These were not very likely to be of much help to her, if only because they resided at considerable distances from here—Atlantes in his famous Iron Castle atop the Pyrenees, which were down in Spain or in whatever country corresponded to Spain in Terra Magica, and Dame Pirouetta beneath a mysterious pool somewhere in the enchanted forest of Broceliande. Callipygia was not at all certain where the enchanted forest was.

"And, if Mandricardo has only been magically transported somewhere. . . ." The girl scowled, thinking deeply. If her lover had been transported somewhere, he would by now be bending every effort to rejoin her, Callipygia. That being the case, presumably the best idea would be for her to simply continue journeying along the route they had planned to follow to distant Tartary. Either her lover would manage to catch up with her at some point along the way, or, when she got back to the Country of the Amazons—and you had to pass through the Country of the Amazons in order to get to Tartary—she could ask one of the friendly sorcerers of Amazonia to find and return him to her side.

Callipygia thought this idea over from every side, and could at length think of no better solution to her problem. She could have gone hunting for the Troll, of course, hoping to catch or trap the creature and then to

force it to undo the spell it had cast on Mandricardo
. . . but it is really not very wise to go making a
nuisance of yourself by badgering creatures with magical powers, and if she tried it, the Troll could simply
use its magic against her, and what good would she be
to Mandricardo then, if she was transformed into a
toadstool or transported to Timbucktoo?

So she rode east, leaving the Troll's cave-door open
so the creature could return at will to its abode. Just in
case Mandricardo managed to get himself transported
back to it, she had written a message with a lump of
charcoal on the Troll's wall for him.

It read:

Dear Mandri,
Hope you have only been transported somewhere
and not turned into a toadstool. I am heading east
for Amazonia. Feeling just fine. Hoping you are
the same,

Yours truly,
Callipygia F.

By midday, she and her horse and the litle baggage
mule paused for lunch at the hut of a poor wood-cutter.
His old wife had been stirring an iron pot of potato and
cabbage soup when the Amazonian princess came riding up, and the couple were than happy to share the
delicious-smelling stuff, together with some black bread
and a couple of raw onions, with their unexpected
guest—and even happier when she paid them with a
pigeon's-blood ruby as big as the skull of a house cat.
When she rode off, the two were happily arguing as to
whether they ought to buy a counthood or a marquisage
with their bounty.

She would probably not have paid them so much for

the meal, but to tell the truth she had nothing smaller on her.

"By Theseus' Toenails, that tasted good!" the girl said to herself. With a tummy full of hot cabbage and potato soup, she felt fit to ride the length of the world. Not to mention the black bread and onions.

And the length of the world she would have to ride, for Tartary was at the opposite end of the earth from Frankland.

Callipygia, undaunted, pressed on.

The Amazon girl was not accustomed to having adventures all by herself and quite missed her usual companionship. Arimaspia would have come in handy—this was the blond Scythian princess whom they had rescued and Kesrick had recently married—and so would Sir Kesrick, the merry, mischievous red-headed knight with his sparkling green eyes and enchanted sword. Of course, it was Mandricardo that she missed most; but there was no good to be gained by brooding over the fact that he no longer rode at her side. She must keep a stiff upper lip and press on. The quicker she got to Amazonia, the sooner she would be able to enlist some friendly magician to her cause.

But it certainly was *boring*, riding along all by herself with nobody to talk to, nobody even to sing with. Mandricardo had possessed a decent tenor voice, she fondly and wistfully recalled. True, all the songs he knew were wild Tartarean drinking and hunting songs, but they were better than nothing. For a time, Callipygia sang to herself an old Amazon hunting song, but somehow her voice sounded lonely and lost amidst the gaunt wet black trunks of the trees, and she let the song lapse into silence.

The good thing about Terra Magica, one good thing, anyway, is that the place is so full of surprises. It's hard

to get bored and to stay bored for very long because
something unexpected is always happening to you.

Like the precipice, when Callipygia came to it.

She had been happy when the forest thinned out and
was left behind. While the countryside was still deep in
fresh-fallen white snow, and there were no huts or
hovels or houses in sight and not even a road to follow,
the Amazon girl felt more comfortable out in the open
country where wolves and monsters and things cannot
creep up on you by hiding behind trees or bushes
before they pounce.

Now, as she rode up to the brink of the enormous
crevasse, she wished she were still in a forest. At least
you can ride through a forest: no one she knew could ride
across thin air. And thin air was exactly what stretched
from one edge of the precipice to the other edge. At
least forty feet of it.

"Now, by Hercules' Hangnail, we *do* have a problem!" the Amazon girl declared in harsh tones. She slid
down from the saddle and went out to the very edge of
the precipice and shuddered. It was very deep and too
broad to jump over. Much too broad. If you or I had
been in her shoes (well, buskins, actually) we might
very well have been reminded of the Grand Canyon,
but this comparison could not have occurred to Callipygia,
since in Terra Magica the Grand Canyon had not as yet
been discovered.*

Callipygia turned and looked north. In that direction,
the crevasse extended as far as her eyes could see,
maybe all the way to Hyperborea or to Cimmeria or to
the Frozen Sea, or whatever was north of here. And
south the same discouraging vista met her gaze; how far

*Actually, I'm not at all sure that Terra Magica even has a Grand Canyon; this
world next door to our own seems to be flat as a plate, with edges over which
you can fall, which implies that it certainly doesn't have a Western Hemisphere
waiting for some Colombus to come along and discover it.

the crevasse extended in either direction she could not guess, but it certainly seemed extensive. And as far as she could tell, it didn't get any narrower in either direction.

The girl scowled again. She looked at her horse, and the red mare looked blandly back at her. She exchanged a long look with the fat little gray mule, Minerva, which frisked her tail from side to side in friendly fashion. Then Callipygia climbed back in the saddle, and turned the mare's nose about until she was heading north.

"Well, we'll see what it's like in this direction, girls," she said grimly.

They rode north about two miles, and found nothing: no bridge, nor anything that could be used for a bridge, like a fallen tree trunk lengthy enough to bridge the gap between this side of the canyon and the far side.

Nor did it narrow appreciably; a little maybe, but the width was still too great to attempt to jump across. And it was a long way down.

Callipygia stopped her mare and sat the saddle, staring moodily at the uncooperative crevasse. The great obstinate thing (she thought, twisting the bronze ring about her upper arm fretfully), would it never come to an end?

How much further north was she supposed to ride? Or should she give up riding in this direction and head south for a league or so? How in the world did people get from one side of that great gaping trench to the other in these parts?

Twisting the ring on her arm, Callipygia snapped: "Oh, I wish we were a thousand miles away from this dismal place!"

And in the next split-second of time, of course, she, her horse and the little gray mule had vanished into thin air.

4

Unexpected Hazards of Tourism

The city, like all Eastern cities, Mandricardo supposed, was very different from those of his experience in that the buildings enclosed gardens and clumps of palms and fountains of sparkling water. The breeze was scented by these secluded gardens, fragrant with citron and jasmine and lime blossoms. Above walls set with tiles of rigid geometric designs in indigo, canary, and vermilion, soared spires and minarets. Swelling domes of burnished copper seemed to float like captive balloons above the fretted alabaster walls of palaces.

Beneath these glittering heights, crooked alleys meandered between walls of plastered stone or brick; gorgeous carpets hung from screened balconies; emirs and nabobs and viziers went by on immense waddling elephants, attended by clattering troops of fierce-looking soldiery. Stalls in the bazaar displayed brassware, onions, kegs of cinnamon, samovars, lacquer bowls, scimitars, rubies, jade ornaments, bales of silken stuff and rich brocade, coconuts, almonds, chunks of amber from

the shores of the Frozen Sea, green peppers, logs of
teak and cedar, silver ingots, pearls.

There seemed no end to the variety of people within
the walls. Noble ladies, veiled to the eyelids, rode
litters borne on the shoulders of brawny servants. Starved
beggars displaying running sores and gaping eye-sockets
clamored for alms. Skinny fakirs in ragged loinclouts
coaxed sommnolent cobras from their baskets by tootling on wooden flutes. Dancing-girls undulated their
bare tummies to the thump and pitter of small drums;
yellow topazes twinkled in their navels. Fat merchants
squabbled and haggled, boasting the rarity of their wares.

Many there were who stared at Mandricardo as the
huge Tartar ambled curiously about, ogling the sights.
The friendly Sheikh had directed him to a caravanserai
where he had obtained lodgings for himself and room in
the stables for Bayardetto; now he strolled the streets
at his leisure, exploring. From booths he purchased
sizzling shish-kebabs, a delicacy previously unsampled
by him; and toasted almonds, heated in brass bowls
over coals that pulsed like rubies; and syrupy coffee or
perfumed fruit-juices or sherbets.

Towering by half a foot and more above the smaller
Paynims of the desert city, Mandricardo had little to
fear from cutpurse or footpad. His impressive inches,
and the length of his great sword which he wore prominently displayed, lent him a certain immunity from the
more prudent and cautious members of the criminal
classes.

Through the midst of the city a vast river glided, slow
silvery flood sliding under the moon. Its broad wrinkled
surface bore innumerable small boats: fishing-craft,
ferries, pleasure-boats, merchanters and the like. From
here to the Delta of the river the shipping was brisk, and
on one such craft the Tartar knight hoped to obtain
passage oversea for himself and horse. Dashed pity that

Mare Nostrum—"Our Sea"—lay between here and the
famous Kingdom of the Franks, but there you are, he
thought to himself. It was not the first time that
Mandricardo had crossed the sea from Afric, but on
that earlier expedition he had enjoyed the companionship of Kesrick of Dragonrouge, Princess Arimaspia,
and his betrothed. Now he was alone, and it was up to
him to bargain and bicker for his passage.

Or should he attempt to return to Frankland at all, he
wondered to himself. Would Callipygia remain there,
awaiting his return, or would she have pressed on
east, toward her own homeland, which lay along the
road to the Kingdom of the Tartars? It was a difficult
question to resolve; he stored it away for further thought
and continued exploring the exotic city.

Storytellers were fountains of volubility on street corners, holding rapt crowds of fascinated boys and
nodding elders, who puffed on curious water-pipes.
Mandricardo lingered on the outskirts of the audience
of one such, who was extolling the adventures of a
certain Prince Camaralzaman, the son of King Schahza-
man, who wooed and wed the daughter of the Emperor
of China through the good offices of a friendly peri
named Maimoune and a genie called Danhasch. The
other listeners seemed familiar with the tale, but it was
new to Mandricardo. The tale would probably have
been familiar to you, too, had you been there: alas,
Mandricardo had never had the opportunity to read the
Arabian Nights.

Mandricardo's venture into tourism took a turn for the
dangerous a few moments after this. He had ambled
away from the crowd that was listening to the profes-
sional storyteller and was going around a corner which
opened upon one of the major thoroughfares of the
desert metropolis. Directly ahead of the Tartar there

waddled a fat, short little merchant in fantastically striped pantaloons, with a towering and tasseled fez of dark red felt a foot tall. By the side of the merchant a bony beggar limped along on a wooden crutch, his alms-bowl tucked under one naked arm.

Quite suddenly, both men stopped short as if they had run into a stone wall which was, for some reason, viewless as the air itself to the eyes of Mandricardo. Without a moment's hesitation, the fat merchant flung himself into the dust, his fez flying across the street, and did his very best to dig his nose into the crevice between two cobblestones—at least, that's what it looked like he was doing.

As for the half-naked beggar, he also hurled himself prone and dug *his* nose into the dust, his small and bony rump thrust skyward. Mandricardo halted his progress and stood staring down at the two. Then the tramp of marching feet came to his ears and he looked up to see a procession of sorts advancing toward him down the broad boulevard; first came spearmen with ring-mail shirts jingling and jangling to the rhythm of their tread, then a troop of mounted archers astride prancing Arab steeds with copper bells woven in their flowing manes, and behind all this there came on ponderous pads a pachyderm with a lacquered howdah strapped atop its swaying back, wherein reposed a thin, gaudily robed personage with a tall green turban from which floated snowy egret-plumes. He had a long and warty nose, rather like a pickle. The elephant he rode was either naturally albino, or had been whitewashed; its tusks had been sawn off short and capped with balls of red gold; earrings as huge as soup-bowls hung from immense, flapping ears.

Mandricardo clasped his hands behind his back and drank in the sight with appreciation; seldom had the Tartar knight enjoyed the opportunity to gawp like a tourist during his travels and adventures—usually things were happening too fast in his immediate vicinity to afford him the leisure to take in the sights—and he meant to repair this omission while he could.

Unfortunately, the wandering and supercilious gaze of the sneering occupant of the howdah, as it flitted about the street, noting with intense pleasure the fawning and supplicating prostrations of everyone in sight except for his entourage (for everyone else on the boulevard was flat on his stomach with his nose buried in the dust), eventually encountered the distinctly erect and *un*prostrate figure of Mandricardo. His guileless gaze met that of the astounded vizier, for the elephant-riding celebrity was none other, I'm sorry to say, than the Grand Vizier of the realm. Alone in a sea of *salaams*, the strapping Tartar stood on his two booted feet, drinking in the spectacle.

The Grand Vizier turned pale, then purpled. He pointed a finger that shook with rage until it resembled an aspen in the wind. From his bearded lips there burst a torrent of abuse, mostly centering about the figure of the impudent and scurrilous foreigner who had rudely and scandalously failed to prostrate himself as the mighty Vizier passed in ceremonial procession. Amidst the hissing, stuttering, stammering flow of speech could be discerned mentions of the bastinado, and more than one reference to boiling-in-oil.

The spearmen stopped in mid-tramp and about-faced, leveling their javelins. The mounted archers turned their steeds about and began selecting arrows to fit to their bows.

In less time that it would take to tell of it, the lot of them were hot on the heels of the hapless tourist, who went pelting down the nearest alley, running for his life.

About a half hour later, breathing rather heavily and

red in the face from his exertions, Mandricardo ducked
into the shop of a carpet-monger. He had managed to
elude the troop of spearmen, who could not run as fast
as he because of their long mailshirts. But the archers
(who had spread out and were busily combing the entire quarter) were of greater agility. And Mandricardo
hoped to lose them amidst the mounds of stacks of
heaped carpets which filled the interior of the shop.

He dove behind one pile of carpets and burrowed
into it until only the tip of his nose remained exposed to
the open air, so that he could continue to breathe.
Then he strove to remain quiet and to calm his thumping heart. As heroic as the next knight-errant, Mandricardo was yet prudent enough to refrain from trying
to engage thirty mounted archers in single-handed combat. He had by now a hazy notion of his trespass against
the local traffic regulations, and realized too late that
when the Grand Vizier went by on elephant-back, the
populace were supposed to flop on their tummies in the
street. Well, by Jove, they should have placards to that
effect posted about, so that strangers could be advised
of the fact, dash it all!

He lay concealed behind the mound of carpets for an
interminable period of time. At length he deemed it
safe enough to emerge to open air again, for surely by
now the archers had long since ridden past the shop of
the carpet-monger. He began to dig himself out—only
to freeze and remain in his place of concealment. For
someone had just entered the rear of the shop where he
lay hidden.

Peering around a corner of the mound of rugs,
Mandricardo perceived a tall, lean individual enveloped
in robes of rusty black, with an ungainly purple turban
perched atop his bony head. His eyes were cold and
black as beads of frozen ink and his mouth was thin,
lipless, and down-curved like the edge of a scimitar. An

aigrette of opals was clipped to the front of his turban. He wore Persian slippers whose toes curled up like the runners on a sled.

Peering about as if to ascertain that his actions were undisturbed, the black-robed personage at length satisfied himself on that point and began digging behind another stack of carpets, fortunately not the one behind which our fugitive Tartar was crouched. At length, the searcher came up with a roll of carpet, which he unrolled before a large and open window which gave forth on a melancholy vista of neglected garden in which unwatered palms drooped their shriveled fronds disconsolately and dusty fountains offered splashless bowls to the noon.

The carpet itself was nothing much to look at and certainly not in the same class as the gorgeous specimens arrayed about on every side. It was faded and frayed and very dusty, and even patched here and there, and what the carpet-monger (if the black-robed individual was, in fact, the carpet-monger whose shop this was) would want with such an inferior and worn-out example of the carpet-makers' craft was beyond the wits of Mandricardo to perceive.

The answer to that question became quite obvious a moment later when the man in the black robe stepped in the middle of the carpet, intoned "Fly, carpet!" in deep tones, and promptly flew out of the window.

5

The Abduction of Doucelette

Mandricardo was flabbergasted. The Tartar knight (could you have seen him at that moment) exhibited every one of the signs of, ah, flabbergastion. That is, his eyes goggled, his jaw dropped, and he tottered, listing heavily to the right, not unlike a suddenly uprooted elm. It took our hero a few moments to recover from his astonishment, but his knightly enthusiasm for magical adventures soon overcame his amazement, and he beamed with bliss.

"I say," marveled Mandricardo, "jolly good show! Ruddy old Magic Flying Carpet, 'pon my word! I've heard of them . . . King Solomon, and all that rot! Well, after all, same part of the world, this." Emerging from behind the stack of carpets, he went over to the open window and peered out into the sad, neglected garden. It afforded him, he rather fancied, a means of escape form the shop without being seen from the street, where, quite possibly, the Grand Vizier's armed henchmen might still be lurking about and on the lookout for a tallish Tartar. Perhaps he could climb yonder trellis to the top and then escape over the roofs of the city, until he reached a spot sufficiently distant from this to afford him security from angry Viziers.

As he considered the stratagem, his eye alighted upon a dark mote traveling through the hot blue sky and seeming to grow larger, evidently approaching his coign of vantage. With alacrity, the Tartar knight dove back into his hidey-hole behind the mound of carpets, and not a moment too soon. For a half-instant later, the faded and dusty old carpet came gliding back through the open windows again, bearing the tall, lean man in the purple turban.

But now the carpet had *another* passenger, and this was a beautiful young Princess in a ball gown of pale green silk! She had enormous masses of rich red-gold hair, caught up in a silken net whose meshes were woven with tiny seed-pearls; her eyes were as green as her gown and formed a delectable contrast with her red hair, and a tiny coronet of gold filigree was held atop her head by hairpins of carven emeralds.

She was bound hand and foot, Mandricardo was interested to see, and her mouth was gagged, so that all she could manage to say were inarticulate, muffled things like "Oomph!" and "Murghgl!"

As soon as the carpet settled to the floor, which it did, every bit as lightly as a floating feather borne along by the breeze, the enchanter—(for what else could he be but an enchanter? Your common or garden variety rug-merchant seldom peregrinates about on Magic Flying Carpets)—the enchanter, I say, hopped off and carried the captive Princess to a corner, where he deposited her unceremoniously on the floor and stood, arms folded, sneering down at her furious glare.

"There, my proud beauty! Just let me close up my shop and you and I will discuss our impending nuptials, which will be celebrated before the Imam at the nearest Mosque whether you will or nill!" And with those sneering words, the man in the purple turban stalked from the room. In a moment you could hear him from the street, shooing away prospective customers and rattling down the blinds to close his shop.

Mandricardo immediately popped up from behind the mound of carpets, behind which he had been hiding and behind which he was by this time rather heartily sick of hiding, and came over to where the redheaded girl lay, staring at him wide-eyed. With his falchion he severed the ropes that bound her limbs and plucked the kerchief from her mouth.

Then he made a courtly bow and lent his arm, assisting the Princess to her feet. "I am hight Sir Mandricardo, son of King Agricane of Tartary, you know," he announced, in the approved chivalric manner. "Damsel in distress, I'll wager! Well, my trusty blade and I are ever at the service of damsels in distress, what?"

Recovering her aplomb, the redheaded girl made a low curtsy to her rescuer. "I am hight the Princess Doucelette of Upper Pamphyllia," she said demurely. "And very grateful for your courtesy in rescuing me from durance vile. I have no doubt that my royal father, King Umberto, will settle upon you my hand in marriage and half of his kingdom, when you return me safely to Court!"

"Good show," said Mandricardo. "Uh, sorry, I'm already promised to the daughter of the Queen of the Amazons, you know, but thank you very much anyway, I'm sure."

"Not at all," said Doucelette politely, with a friendly smile which revealed as delectable a brace of dimples as ever graced a maidenly cheek. She hadn't really wanted to marry Mandricardo particularly, especially not upon such short acquaintance, but these things are done according to *a certain form*, you know.

"So your father is hight King Umberto, eh?" said the Tartar chattily. "My pater is hight King Agricane, but I've already mentioned that, 'pon my soul! What is that enchanter hight, by the way, ma'm, if you don't mind me askin'?"

The Princess shuddered fastidiously. "He is an unprincipled caitiff rogue and varlet," she explained primly, "and he calls himself the enchanter Gorgonzola."

"Uncouth sort of name, that," murmured Mandricardo reflectively.

"Quite," said the Princess. "He has placed all of my father's kingdom under a dire and dismal Curse, which he will only remove if my father will bestow upon him my hand!" She shuddered again, in mere contemplation of what might well be termed a Fate Worse Than Death.

"The blighter!" snorted Mandricardo, eyes aflash and moustaches abristle with outrage. "To inflict himself, all unwanted, upon a delicately-nurtured damsel! By my halidom, but words fail me!"

"I *quite* understand your sentiments, sir knight," said Doucelette, casting an apprehensive gaze in the direction of the door which led to the front of the shop, "but perhaps we should flee before the Enchanter returns and discuss these matters later, once we are safe. . . ?"

"Good thinkin', begad!" said Mandricardo, striding over to the window. "What say we climb that ruddy trellis to the roof, and make our escape, what, over the rooftops. . . ?"

Doucelette cleared her throat daintily.

"Eh, what?"

"Why don't we fly off on the Magic Flying Carpet, which the vile caitiff rogue and varlet has unwittingly left at our disposal?" suggested the girl in practical terms. "To do so would not only give us a mode of rapid aerial conveyance, but would rob our pursuer of his magical flying vehicle, forcing him (should he prove so relentless as to attempt our pursuit) to plod along on foot while we fly upon the wings of the wind."

"Er, ah," said Mandricardo nervously.

"Here, just stand in the center beside me," suggested Doucelette, taking her place.

"Ah, um, er," remarked Mandricardo. He was *not really fond* of flying, and much preferred to have either his or his horse's feet solidly on the ground at all times, as often as possible. Still and all, the Princess's idea was obviously the only thing to do. Reluctantly, spurs ajingle, he strode upon the carpet, and stood at Doucelette's side.

"I say, Carpet, you may commence," said Mandricardo in forceful tones, eyes squeezed tightly shut. A moment later, he said in a small voice, "I say, ma'm, are we, ah, *aloft* yet?"

They were not. And from the front of the shop came clearly the sounds of thumps and rattles and bangs as Gorgonzola the Enchanter let down the striped awnings, rolled up his carpets, stowed safely away the boxes and baskets and bales, and made haste to close down the carpet-shop for the day.

"Come, Carpet, you great ninny!" roared Mandricardo, scarlet in the face, petulantly stamping one booted foot. "Fly, blast you!"

Again, Princess Doucelette cleared her throat politely.

"I believe the operative phrase, sir knight, is 'Fly, Carpet!' " she said.

"Eh? Oh, really? Well, why didn't you say so before? Can't stand here all day long, talkin' to carpets, what? Fly, Carpet! . . . *Oh, my!*"

Shaking itself slightly, the Carpet floated up off the ground and zoomed through the open window. It took a tight turn around a withering palm and soared above the building into the fierce blaze of the early afternoon sun.

"Ker-hem!" snorted Sir Mandricardo; beneath his Tartarian swarthiness he had gone pale and was, in fact, just a trifle green about the lips, eyes squeezed shut. The Princess tugged at the lion-skin which he wore over one armored shoulder.

"Where shall we go, sir knight? Do you mean to return me to my father's Court, or have you missions of your own upon which you were bound, when the necessity of effecting my rescue from that unscrupulous varlet interrupted your quest?"

"Got to return to the inn, dash it all, I mean caravanserai, and pick up me horse," said Mandricardo, prying one eyelid open briefly, "as well as gettin' away from that white elephant chappie."

"Which white elephant chappie?" inquired Doucelette.

"Chap ridin' on a white elephant," explained Mandricardo. "When I didn't flop down on my face before the blighter, he sicced his soldiers on me. Mean-lookin' sod; nose like a pickle."

"I believe you refer to the Grand Vizier," murmured Doucelette. "I happened to see his likeness painted in miniature once, and he did indeed have a nose like a pickle. Where is your horse?"

"Beg pardon?"

"Your *horse*; where is your horse. We are over the Delta by now, and heading for open sea," said the Princess.

It took the two of them more than a little time to get the Magic Flying Carpet turned about and to send it back in the correct and proper direction, and not until it came floating down as lightly as a leaf in the courtyard behind the caravanserai—sending geese squawking

in all directions and severely discomforting a brace of
goats—did Mandricardo open his eyes again.

While the Tartar knight paid his bill in the caravanserai, finding that a plump pigeon's-blood ruby went a
long way in the local currency, for his change was a bag
full of gold dinars big enough to choke a hippo (if a
hippo could be induced to try to swallow a bag full of
dinars), the stableboy curried Bayardetto and saddled
him and led the black stallion out of the stable to be
introduced to the Princess of Upper Pamphyllia. (She
slipped him a carrot and they became fast friends.)

Mandricardo measured the three of them, then stared
at the dilapidated piece of carpet for comparison. He
shook his head despairingly.

"Don't think we'll all fit on the Magic Flyin' Carpet,
ma'm," he opined. "Ruddy thing's just not big enough."

"Let's try it, anyway, sir knight," suggested the Princess. She had always heard that Magic Flying Carpets
can stretch themselves to any size in order to accommodate their passengers; this was indeed the case, as they
discovered. The Carpet rippled, blurred, became large
enough for knight, charger, and Princess. It reminded
Mandricardo of a similar experience concerning a magic
boat called Skidbladnir which he had encountered during an earlier adventure.

They mounted the Carpet and took off for Pamphyllia.
It was Mandricardo's notion to first fly Princess Doucelette home to the safety of her father's Court, then off
to Frankland or wherever, hoping to locate his beloved
Amazon.

"Suppose this is one of King Solomon's magic flyin'
carpets, eh, what?" he murmured after a time (they
were flying over the Suez Canal, or where the Suez
Canal would be if Terra Magica possessed one, which it
did not). However, the *Chronicle Narrative* does not
make it clear whether he referred to the King Solomon

of the Old Testament, or to Soliman Djinn-ben-Djinn, mightiest of the seventy-two pre-Adamite Sultans. As the next line of dialogue renders the point irrelevant, I will not attempt to speculate.

"No, not to him, but to his maiden aunt, Zuleika," replied the redheaded Princess. "That infamous rogue Gorgonzola could not resist boasting to me of the rarity and value of our mode of conveyance, after completing his odious mission of abducting my person from the grounds of my father's palace. I was helping the goosegirl pick blueberries for a pie," she added absently.

"I say, did the beggar explain why he was pretendin' to be a carpet-monger?" asked Mandricardo. Doucelette shook her head, making her little gold filigree coronet twinkle in the westering sun.

"No, and I had no reason to think him one until he landed the Magic Flying Carpet in the back room of a carpet-shop," she said. "However, one supposes that even wicked enchanters have to do *something* to make a living, having their enchantery as a sort of hobby on the side, don't you think?"

"Deuced clever," mused Mandricardo. "*I'd* never have thought of that."

Bayardetto neighed and whickered just then: they had flown through a very low-flying cloud, and the sudden immersion in cold wet mist tickled all of their nostrils. On the whole, you rather had to admire Bayardetto's *savoir-faire*. Surely, only a strictly limited number of warhorses have ever enjoyed the opportunity to ride about on Magic Flying Carpets, so the experience must have been quite a novelty for him. Even without the benefits of hereditary instinct to support him during this rather unnerving experience, the stallion managed everything with commendable aplomb.

It began to get rather dark rather quickly. Aloft where they were flying, the level and ruddy shafts of sanguinary sunlight still bathed them, but beneath their keel (so to speak) the landscape was steeped in the shadows as in the purple lees of wine.

And they were getting hungry.

"Just how far is it to Upper Pamphyllia, m'am, about?" queried Mandricardo. "Never been there, meself." He was beginning to get used to flying; the experience was not all that frightening once you became accustomed to it, he found. Many others, on their maiden flights, have discovered the same thing.

"As the Carpet flies?" said Doucelette with a smile at her little joke. "Actually, sir knight, I've no idea. When we flew from there to Aegypt, well, as you can imagine, I was *that* annoyed and upset—"

"No wonder; wicked enchanter and all; kidnapping, what?" murmured Mandricardo understandingly.

"Quite. You *do* understand, Sir Mandricardo! As I say, I was simply too upset to pay much attention to the passing of time, but surely it can't be very much longer. There's Troy off to the side there, you can recognize it by the topless towers, and before long we should be able to spy Colchis where they used to keep the Golden Fleece—"

They flew on into the dusk.

BOOK TWO

Salamandre
and Undina

6

A Very Damp Knight

Callipygia uttered a stifled squeak and bit her tongue. Then she squeezed her eyes shut, cautiously opened one, took a quick peek around, and hastily closed it again.

She was no longer standing on the pebble-strewn brink of the impassable chasm. Now she was knee-deep in the lush grasses of a green meadow. Trees marched along the horizon, congregating atop low hummocky hills. Also, no longer was the day blindingly clear: now it was dim and gloomy, under a sky thronged with a turbulence of moist dark vapors.

Either she had been transported to another place, or the landscape itself had undergone a miraculous transformation, chasm into meadow, sunny sky to gloom. And the transportation, if that is really what it was, had been performed in an eye-blink. There had been no slightest sensation of movement or velocity. She let her breath out slowly and pried her eyes open.

Both the red mare and the plump little gray mule,

Minerva, were adversely affected by the feat of magic
that had brought them all here to this unknown spot.
The horse and the mule rolled their eyes in panicky
fashion, ears laid flat along their skulls, and the horse
neighed while the mule brayed.

"It's all right, girls, nothing to worry about," murmured the Amazon girl in soothing tones, patting them
in an attempt to comfort them. Inwardly, of course, the
warrior girl was saying, "What in the name of Memnon's
Moustache *happened?*"

No answer came to mind. Erelong she had soothed
the beasts, mounted up, and tried to figure out which
direction was which. There was no easy way to tell
since the sun was hidden behind a blanket of wooly
clouds, and nowhere in sight did she perceive a town or
city or any other token of humanity.

"Magic again," she said grimly to herself. But not the
Troll, surely; they had been hours away from the Troll's
woods when magic had struck again. And again Callipygia
racked her mind to think of some powerful enchanter
who might have it in for her and Mandricardo; no name
rose to mind.

"Not Grumedan, surely, and everybody else is either
dead or transfixed to stone," she muttered to herself.
Thumping her heels in the mare's ribs, she turned the
horse's nose toward a distant stand of trees and followed
the road that led in that direction, more to be moving
than for any particular desire to travel there. "When in
doubt, keep moving!" was Callipygia's motto.

All this magic happening was beginning to get on the
Amazon's nerves. True, it was good to have gotten away
from that dreadful crevasse, but at least there she had
known where she was, after all. Here, she had no idea:
this could be the empire of Prester John for all she
knew.

The stand of trees happened to be pear trees, as it

turned out, and several ripe pears still clung to their
parental branches. Callipygia unsaddled her mare and
removed the saddlebags from Minerva, and permitted
the two now-unburdened creatures to wander at will
along the edge of the meadow and dine off the lush
green grasses, while she munched on a slab of cheese
from her stores and chewed thirstily on the luscious
fruits.

Wherever they were, it was nowhere near as cold as
it had been back in the northerly parts of the kingdom
of the Franks. And although those lowering clouds hinted
of rain, the breeze was too warm and moist to be
redolent of snow. They must have been transported a
sizable distance, to have changed their climate this
much, thought Cally.

"Well, let's just hope we're east of where we were,"
she sighed aloud after a bit. "At least we'd be moving in
the right direction." She prowled through the little
stand of trees, emerging on the other side to find herself on the edge of a lake of considerable extent. It
gleamed dully, pewter-colored under the gloomy gray
sky.

"*Halloo-o-o!*"

The distant call was repeated while the Amazon girl
stared around, searching the landscape for the origin of
the cry. At length she spied a young man in armor
waving his arms frantically in an attempt to catch her
eye.

"Halloo yourself," called Cally. "What are you doing
in the middle of that lake?" The young knight (for that's
what he seemed to be) stood atop a tiny hummock
exactly in the center of the lake before her.

"I'm marooned, madam, I'm afraid," he called back.
"Do you think . . . is there anything you can do to get
me off this hummock?"

Cally looked around briefly. There were no rafts or rowboats in sight, so she shook her head.

"How did you get out there in the first place?" she called. "In the middle of the lake, I mean."

"There wasn't any lake here when I got here," he called back. Then he began coughing. "If you don't mind," said the knight as soon as he had ceased coughing, "I'll just save my explanations until I get off this islet. All of this shouting back and forth is giving me a sore throat, or would be giving me one, if I didn't already have one from standing around in wet clothes and soggy boots. Can't you get me of this filthy hummock somehow?"

"How, exactly, do you suggest?" called Callipygia.

"Can't you swim?"

"As a matter of fact, no, I can't," said Callipygia. The country of the Amazons is in the interior, and there are no lakes worth mentioning and even the rivers are rather shallow, so she had never had cause or opportunity to learn that invaluable skill.

"Can't *you?*" she called.

"As a matter of fact, no, I can't," he replied woefully, heaving a rather squishy sigh. "Well, I guess I might as well sit down in all this wet mud and catch my death of cold. If you think of anything, just yell."

"I will, be of good cheer," said Callipygia. She went back through the little grove of pear trees, plucking a few more ripe ones to put in her wallet. Then she collected Minerva and the red mare—the mare's name was Blondel, by the way—and led them through the trees to the edge of the lake.

It was fresh water, so all three drank therefrom while the poor damp knight (and he really did look all wet and squishy) watched them sadly from his muddy little hummock.

"I say, could you at least toss me a pear?" he called

when they had finished drinking. "I've been here since early this morning and by this time I am quite famished."

Callipygia was nothing loath, if nothing loath means what I think it means. The first couple of pears landed in the drink, but after that the Amazon girl managed to land them more precisely, and soon the damp knight was munching hungrily on the juicy fruit.

"I am hight Prince Florizel, by the way," he said. "The son of King Rumberto of Lower Pamphyllia."

Callipygia jumped, which is rather hard to do, come to think of it, when you are sitting down, and she was sitting down at the time.

"Lower Pamphyllia!" she exclaimed in excited tones. "Why, by Apollo's Eyelids, but that country is a thousand miles away from the northerly parts of the famous Kingdom of the Franks!"

"I believe it is," agreed Prince Florizel curiously, "but why does that occasion such excitement in you, and by the way, what are you hight, anyway?"

"Oh, sorry! I am hight the Princess Callipygia, one of the seventeen daughters of Queen Megamastaia of Amazonia. How do you do."

"How do *you* do," said Florizel politely. "I have never happened to meet an Amazon before."

"Well, there are plenty of us around, at least in Amazonia . . . anyway," continued Callipygia, picking up the thread of the conversation again, "I was so excited because just before I came here a little while ago, I was wishing myself to be a thousand miles away from where I was, which happened to be in the northerly parts of the famous kingdom of the Franks. And *zip-zoop!* here I was! Here I am, I mean."

"That's odd."

"Isn't it odd? Almost as if I had traveled here on a wish, or something."

"Yes, it certainly sounds like a wish. You don't hap-

pen to have a wishing ring about you anywhere, on
your person, I mean?" inquired Florizel. From the
expression on his rather long and melancholy face, which
had sad brown eyes and limp, dripping hair, it was
apparent that he was thinking that if Callipygia had
happened to have a wishing ring on her somewhere, on
her person, that is, she could easily wish him to dry
land and out of the middle of that lake.

"I'm afraid not," said Callipygia. "Pity you can't swim."

He heaved a deep sigh. "Isn't it? If I stay here
tonight, I'll have caught my death of cold by morning."
He attempted a rather half-hearted cough or two. She
looked sympathetic.

"Well . . . is there a town around here anywhere?"
she asked. "Where I might borrow a rowboat or a raft
or something."

"Well, of course, right back at the other end of the
road you were following," he said with some slight as-
perity. "You had to go through the center of the village
in order to get here . . . oh. Sorry. I forgot; you *did* say
you had traveled here on a wish, or something?"

"Or something," nodded Callipygia.

Well, there was a town all right, just as Florizel had
predicted, and it proved possible to rent a rowboat
there, although the man who rented it to Callipygia was
powerfully mystified when she asked him to fetch it out
in the countryside for her. He naturally expected her to
go rowboating in the small river that meandered through
the village, not out in the middle of dry fields. When
he saw the lake, however, he seemed to understand all
too well.

"Lor' lumme, not another *lake!*" he groaned. By the
way, he was named Tozzer, a man of less than medium
height, almost completely surrounded by whiskers.
Through the shrubbery he gazed as if stricken to the

heart at the vista of lake water and hummock and Florizel and all.

"What do you mean, 'another lake'?" demanded Callipygia.

"Why, bless you, yer worship, but that makes three just this week, it do. *Three.*"

"Three what?" she inquired.

The whiskery little man peered at her through the boskage.

"Why, bless yer 'art, ma'm, three new lakes, that's what," he said. "Hold on, now; 'arf a mo'—I'll have yer moist friend out of there in just a jiffy, mebbe two."

And he rowed briskly out into the middle of the lake, leaving Callipygia to puzzle over his mysterious remark. Erelong he returned with the young knight slumped dispiritedly in the rowboat beside him. The young man was every bit as damp up close as he had seemed from a distance.

"Why, dear me, but you're soaking wet!" cried Callipygia. "And that can't be doing your armor any good, not at all."

"Yes ma'm; I mean, no ma'm," sighed the Prince lugubriously. "Ach*oo!*" he added.

Florizel helped the villager load his rowboat back into his cart and mounted up beside him. They rode back to town, Cally clopping along beside them and Minerva trotting behind, still munching a last mouthful of lush meadow grass.

"Reckon yer here on account of the Quest, right, yer worship?" inquired the villager pertly, looking Florizel over from stem to stern, as it were.

"That's right," said Florizel gloomily.

The villager cast a bright, questioning glance at Callipygia, taking in her own abbreviated armor and the short Amazonian sword she wore. His bewhiskered lips parted to ask her the same question.

"I don't know anything about a Quest," said the Amazon girl. "I just happened to be passing through, on my way to the Empire of Tartary, and there he was, high and not-so-very-dry in the middle of a lake. A lake that wasn't there earlier, according to him."

The whiskery villager nodded through the undergrowth. "Yes, just like I sez, third new lake this week. *Dern* that pesky Undina!"

"I'll go along with that, friend," sighed Florizel, moving his feet on the buckboard of the cart. His boots made *squish, squish* noises because each boot contained perhaps a quart of lakewater.

"I wish you'd tell me what you're talking about," complained Callipygia, rather frostily. As the rescuer of Prince Florizel, she felt annoyed at being left out of things. "*What* Quest? What's an Undina? And what do you mean, 'three new lakes just this week'?"

Florizel opened his mouth to answer her, but sneezed instead. Then he sneezed again.

"Double gesundheit," said Callipygia. "Perhaps it can wait until we get to a nice warm inn and sit you down before the fire and pour some nice hot mulled wine or something inside of you."

"That sounds wonderful," said Florizel miserably, wiping his nose.

"*Achoo!*" he added.

7

All About Gorgonzola

Mandricardo and Doucelette had decided to come to
earth for a bit of a meal before continuing on their flight
to Upper Pamphyllia. According to her estimate, they
would not arrive at the palace of her father until past
midnight, and the kitchen would be closed by then and
all the meat cold.

Fortunately, they spied an inn amidst the waste of
sands that undulated beneath their keel (so to speak) in
all directions except for north, where Our Sea could be
seen glinting redly in the last dregs of sunset. As
Mandricardo still had that fat sack of gold dinars, there
was no reason why they should not descend for an early
dinner and then fly on to the capital of Upper Pamphyllia
when they were finished with their meal. It is, after all,
no fun having adventures on an empty stomach; come
to think of it, it is no fun doing much of *anything* on an
empty stomach.

They brought the Magic Flying Carpet to earth in
the courtyard quite unseen, got off, and Mandricardo

rolled it up and stuffed it under Bayardetto's saddle. Then he gave the horse into the care of a stableboy, who gaped at his towering inches and drooping moustaches, and led the Princess into the taproom of the inn.

Mine Host could see at a glance that they were Quality, and though Quality seldom deigned to honor his lowly Establishment with its gracious custom, he hastened to reassure them. The table nearest to the fire was offered them, although that meant dragging two lice-ridden camel-drivers from their comfy seats. A haunch of lamb sizzled, dripping juicily over the roaring fire and filling the smoky air of the inn with delicious odors. Mandricardo ordered slabs of the lamb, dippers of hot spiced gravy and dumplings, steaming tender carrots, and black bread; and they ate heartily, washing the meal down with two bottles of the finest vintage. There is nothing like adventuring to give a man a good appetite, as Mandricardo had often noticed before.

When they had come, if not to a stopping place in their meal, then at least to a place to pause and catch their breaths, Mandricardo questioned his companion: "I say, what about this dashed Enchanter? I mean, caitiff rogue, dragging you off without so much as a how-dee-do, I'll wager! Tell me about the blighter, do."

Doucelette daintly wiped her lips with one of Mine Host's finest cambric napkins and took a sip of the excellent wine.

"I had passed my girlhood in happy innocence of the very existence of the vile Enchanter, Gorgonzola," she began her tale. "It was not until I entered upon my sixteenth year, and that was only a week ago, that the loathsome Gorgonzola impinged upon my attention. He appeared one day at Court, sumptuously mounted and royally attired, announcing himself as some wealthy and powerful emir or nabob from some friendly Eastern realm here a-visiting, and at once began to sue for my hand; in fact, he swore by Mahoum and Golfarin and Termagant that none other than he should win my hand in marriage!"

"You don't say! Very unsporting, what?" observed Mandricardo, critically. The Princess nodded unhappily, and gave a sad little smile that, however sorrowful, was also very entrancing. You see, it displayed her dimples to best advantage. Although he was, of course, bethrothed to Dame Callipygia, his one true love, Mandricardo could not help admiring her smile; it was an impish one, adorned with that brace of dimples; it was not anything that she did knowingly, he thought—it was just the way her face folded.

"Yes; in fact, the Wicked Enchanter even swore (whether it was by Mahoum, or Golfarin, or by Termagant I can't quite recall; perhaps it was by all three of his pagan Idols!) that if he could not have me, then no man ever should!"

And here the Princess shuddered delicately and turned a bit pale.

"The dashed blighter," breathed Mandricardo, bronzed fingers curling about the well-worn hilt of his trusty sword. Nothing so roused his chivalric Tartar blood as to hear of vile Enchanters suing for the hands of innocent damosels, princesses or not.

"Quite," said Doucelett. "My father, King Umberto, felt that I was perhaps a bit too young to become engaged as yet, and anyway had always more or less planned upon making my marriage with the scion of a neighboring kingdom's royal house. So he demurred; but Gorgonzola continued to press his suit; at length, as his attentions became all but intolerable—" and here the Princess shuddered fastidiously.

"Deuced if I'd have put up with it," snorted Mandricardo, his dark eyes flashing sparks of manly fury.

"Quite," said Doucelette. "Nor would my royal father. He sternly bade the Enchanter to depart from Court, never to return until he brought with him on his second visit the manners of a gentleman, which on this first occasion he seemed to have left behind—"

"Oh, jolly good!" applauded Mandricardo, glowing.

"Quite," said Doucelette. "Well, to reduce an interminable narrative to one of more comfortable brevity, Gorgonzola soon departed, rolling his eyes, gnashing his teeth and swearing vile oaths, vowing vengeance upon us all."

"Rotter," said Mandricardo between his teeth.

"To be sure," agreed Doucelette, perhaps wearying of saying "quite" all the time. "Well, to continue, there soon fell a strange and terrible curse upon the kingdom of Upper Pamphyllia. It began with a spell of unseasonably warm weather. Perhaps I should explain, since you have never before visited our kingdom, that we enjoy a moderate climate all year round, but that it does become a trifle cooler during these months of the year."

"Quite," said Mandricardo.

"The warm spell became a hot spell," said Doucelette, twisting her napkin ring sadly. "And the hot spell became tropic in its intensity. The first to be destroyed was our corn crop, upon which much of the prosperity of our kingdom depends; then, in swift succession, as the unbearable torridity continued without abatement, our crops of wheat, barley and sugar-cane succumbed to the heat."

"Good gad!" Mandricardo exclaimed.

"Precisely," said Doucelette. "It was at this point that my royal father summoned the most celebrated wizards, sorcerers, and magicians who made their abode in our realm. One and all they assured him that the unusual spell of tropical warmth was the work of some malign enchantment, and it was one particular seer who

managed, as it were, to lay his finger upon the exact
cause of our hot weather. He said it was the work of a
Salamandre!"

"Deuced Salamandre, eh?" ejaculated Mandricardo.
"Fire elemental, what? No wonder you had all that
warm weather."

"Precisely," said Doucelette. "Now, my royal father
inquired further of the wise men and learned that elemental spirits are by ordinary practice the slaves of
powerful enchanters and not of sorcerers, wizards, or
magicians. Hence, most unfortunately, none of the sorcerers, wizards, or magicians currently gathered at Court
could be expected to help us in our dire predicament
since none of them were enchanters. What we needed
was an enchanter, and the only one who sprang instantly to mind—"

"Was that blighter, Gorgowhatzis," exclaimed Mandricardo, Seeing the Light.

"Precisely," said Doucelette. "The Enchanter himself
appeared at Court not long after this, pretending sor-
row at the curse which had befallen Upper Pamphyllia
and was swiftly blighting our kingdom and reducing its
populace to nigh beggary. He announced himself ready
and willing to employ his enchantments to remove the
curse, if possible, asking only for my hand in marriage—"

"The *cad*," said Mandricardo, bitterly. "Wouldn't be
at all surprised if it wasn't this Gorgowhozit who set the
Salamandre on you in the first place!"

"Such was, in fact, my father's guess," admitted
Doucelette. "So he spurned the Wicked Enchanter and
announced a Quest, hoping for some worthy youth of
royal blood who would be able to lift the Salamandre's
curse from Upper Pamphyllia. Gorgonzola departed in
a magic whirlwind, spitting curses and swearing that
never should the Salamandre depart from the parched
and smoldering fields of Upper Pamphyllia until our

once green and fertile land had been transformed into a burning desert and all of its people reduced to direst poverty. And so the matter stood for the better part of a week."

"Dashed interestin' story, this," nodded Mandricardo. "Ho, landlord—another bottle of your best! Go on, ma'm, do."

"Well, my royal father had naturally expected that the prince of our neighboring realm, which is called Lower Pamphyllia, would quite likely be interested in the Quest. His name," she said with a modest blush, veiling her lovely green eyes behind thick lashes, "is Florizel. Prince Florizel. He is about my own age or just a couple of years older."

"Stout fella, I'm sure," nodded Mandricardo, pouring wine into both their goblets.

"I, ah, happen to know that Prince Florizel—whom I have never met, of course—finds me, ah, interesting. That is because on my sixteenth birthday, just a few weeks ago, my royal father had the celebrated painter Tomaso Lorenzo paint my portrait, which was exhibited widely in foreign capitals. It was, of course, shown in Lower Pamphyllia, where I am given to understand Prince Florizel himself enthused over it. . . ." Here she blushed most becomingly.

"Right-oh! So when this Florizel chappie came to fight the Salamandre, what happened?"

"Nothing happened, I'm sorry to say. Because he never came. Never came at all; and my father sent him a special Quest invitation engraved on the finest stock. . . ."

Her voice trailed away into a snuffle and she looked wistful. Mandricardo grumped and snorted to himself, fingering his clean-shaven and rather swarthy jaw, looking uncomfortable.

"Well, I say, dash it all, path of true love, you know. Never *does* run smooth, as the fella says. Cheer up!"

"Thank you," said the Princess, essaying a rather feeble smile which looked as if her heart was not quite in it. "I know that you are right, but still. . . ."

"So how did you come to get snatched away on the bally old carpet, eh?" asked Mandricardo. The full meal and strong wine and warmth of the fire were all combining to make him sleepy, and the length of Doucelette's tale was not helping any. He felt an almost overpowering urge to turn in and get a good night's sleep. And perhaps that was exactly what they should do . . . they could always arrive at Upper Pamphyllia the next morning, bright and early and ready for Salamandres.

"I guess the villainous Gorgonzola ran out of patience," sighed Doucelette. "All I can say is this morning when I got up and had my bath and dresssed and breakfasted, I went for a stroll in the orange groves in the palace gardens as I always do, to feed the goldfish in the pond and the white peacocks on the lawn and the deer and all. . . ."

"And?"

"And then the goosegirl asked me if I would like to help her pick blueberries for a pie the Cook was making, so I went off with her into that part of the palace gardens, and. . . ."

"And?"

"And there was the Wicked Enchanter, trying to conceal himself behind a blueberry bush! The goosegirl squealed and ran for help, but before I could do more than merely gasp, Gorgonzola whipped a kerchief about my mouth, stifling my cries. Then he bound me hand and foot, using cords he had evidently fetched along with him for just that purpose. He popped me on the Magic Flying Carpet—I didn't know that it was a Magic Flying Carpet at the moment, of course, but it wasn't

very long before I discovered that this is what it was—
and hopped on himself, said, 'Fly, Carpet,' and off we
went!"

"Poor *gel!*" breathed Mandricardo, touched to the
core by this stirring narrative of perils.

And her story finished, the Princess began to snuffle
daintily into her balled-up hanky. Mandricardo made
the usual *tush-tush*ing sounds that men make when
women began to weep, thumped her a time or two
between the shoulder blades and called for the bill.

Assisting her to rise to her feet, the Tartar knight
said: "Well, can't say I understand why this Florizel of
yours is actin' so unknightly, but let's get ourselves a
good night's sleep here and go on to your pater's capital
in the mornin', what? Then we'll see what can be done
about riddin' you Upper Pamphyllians of that dratted
Salamandre of yours."

"We should be ever so obliged, sir knight," Doucelette
assured him. And they set off to see about their rooms.

8

The Water-Maid

When Callipygia and Prince Florizel and the whiskery little man got back to the village, Tozzer directed them to the best inn in town and rode off in his cart to return his rowboat to its little dock in the river. Now that he was gone, Callipygia permitted herself a very un-Amazon-like giggle.

"Did you ever see such whiskers in your *life?*" she asked. "That little man looked like a bush with legs—!"

Florizel smiled feebly and uttered a miserable sniff. Remembering her obligation to the young knight she had just rescued from a watery grave, Cally grabbed him by one arm and steered him into the inn, where they took seats near the huge fire that roared on the grate and he began to pull off his boots, from each of which he poured a quantity of lake-water.

The Amazon girl held a brief negotiation with the landlord of the inn and soon returned bearing a huge earthenware mug which held a quart of hot mulled spiced wine.

"*This* will make you feel like a new man again, by Hercules' Hangnail!" she grinned.

It smelled delicious and steamed fragrantly with heat. Florizel lifted the quart to his lips and when next he lowered it, it was only a pint and he was scarlet in the face and perspiring. Also his eyes were watering.

He said, "*Whoof!*" and put the mug down.

"I added in a few more spices," the Amazon girl informed him. "A handful of powdered cinnamon, half a jug of lemon juice, a few cloves. . . ."

"I know; I can still taste them," he said hoarsely. She helped him drag off his sodden surcoat and spread it out over the end of the table so the fire could begin to dry it.

The landlord brought them platters of raw onions, apples, cheese, black olives, sausages, and a cup of ordinary unmulled wine for Callipygia. Since Florizel had been marooned amidst the mysterious lake all day, the young Prince needed no encouragement. He fell upon the food as a famished wolf falls upon a poor wood-cutter, chance-met in the midst of a wintry forest.

When at length Florizel came back up for air, Callipygia pressed him for the answers to a few questions. Like, what about this Quest, and what did Tozzer mean by "three new lakes just this week," and what was an Undina?

"It's a long story," he said around a mouthful of spicy sausage. "Suffice it to say that a dreadful plague or curse has fallen upon the kingdom of Lower Pamphyllia. This curse is in the form of an Undina—that's a water elemental, the sort of thing conjured up by enchanters, you know."

"Oh," said Callipygia, who hadn't known. "What does the Undina do, exactly?"

"She makes it rain all the time, and even when it isn't actually raining, it's foggy and misty. Everything is moist and dripping all the time—look at me!—and nothing ever seems to get quite dry."

"I see," said Callipygia.

"All of this rain has been ruining our crops," Florizel went on. "The turnips and cabbages are washed right out of the fields, and the wheat is all soggy and rotten; the hens are damp and miserable and so grouchy that they refuse to lay their eggs. The people are getting hungry, and soon there will be famine in the land, and when there is famine, it is usually followed by plague. . . ."

"Um," said Callipygia.

"So my royal father announced a Quest, and offered the half of his kingdom to the knight who managed to destroy or drive away this troublesome pest of an Undina and restore things to normalcy. He would have thrown in the hand of the Princess, except that there isn't any Princess; I have no sisters."

"Ah." This from Callipygia.

"They are also having a plague or curse or something over in the neighboring realm of Upper Pamphyllia, and there they *are* offering the hand of the Princess. Her name is Doucelette. I am firmly convinced that she is the most beautiful girl in the world. At least, she's the most beautiful girl that I've ever seen. Not that I've actually seen her, you understand, just a portrait of her, but it was a genuine Tomaso Lorenzo, and he's supposed to be very good, you know."

"Oh?" said Callipygia.

"Yes; well, anyway, to continue: I was just leaving for Upper Pamphyllia to go on *their* Quest and win the hand of Princess Doucelette if I was lucky, when we began to have all this trouble with the Undina, and my father announced a Quest of our own. Naturally, he hates to divide the kingdom in half so as to split it with whomever manages to kill the Undina, so I, well. . . ."

"It would be better to keep it in the family, is that it?" asked Callipygia. He nodded vigorously, damp hair flopping across his high pale forehead.

"Exactly. So I rode out this morning hoping to find the Undina. And instead, she found me. My horse and squire drowned beneath that lake she made to happen, and I was stuck the whole day long atop that filthy hummock of sloppy mud, catching my death of—ah, ah—" he made the sort of noises people make when they are about to sneeze.

Callipygia shoved another huge steaming mug across the table at him.

"Have some more hot mulled wine," she suggested.

After Florizel had dried out and was feeling much better, with a good lunch inside of him and all that hot mulled wine and everything, the two debated what to do. The spark of chivalric endeavor flamed high in Callipygia's breast, and it just was not in the Amazon girl, having heard this tale of woe, to go riding on toward Tartary and leave the poor Lower Pamphyllians wallowing in their moist doom.

"I suppose if *you* overcome the Undina and achieve the Quest, my royal father will offer you my hand in marriage and half his kingdom and all that," remarked Florizel gloomily, thinking of the slender and willowy charms of Doucelette as compared to the more ample and robust features of Callipygia, but too polite to make his feelings obvious.

The Amazon girl grinned, guessing the direction of his thoughts and really not at all minding the comparison. "Don't be afraid, Sir Florizel," she chuckled, "I have no intentions of getting married. Of getting married to *you*, I mean. I am already betrothed to Sir Mandricardo, the Tartar knight, you see."

"Oh," said Florizel. He sounded relieved.

Then he asked, rather diffidently, "But do you think you can do anything against the Undina?"

She shrugged good-humoredly. "Nothing ventured, nothing gained! Can't say, boy, never having met an Undina before. Let's go and seek her out, shall we? You did say she was a 'she'? We girls have a lot in common, you know; maybe I can persuade her to move somewhere else before she turns all of Lower Pamphyllia into a permanent swamp."

"*Or* an inland sea," added Florizel drearily.

Later that day the two found the Undina, as some farmers had promised they would, amidst another "new lake," this one in a circle of low hills somewhat to the north of where Florizel's first encounter with the water elemental had taken place. They parked their steeds below and crept cautiously up to the skyline and peered over. Someone was singing faintly and off-key.

It was the Undina. Like one of the mermaids she so closely resembled, the fish-girl was seated on a rock combing her long blue-green hair with a bit of comb and peering into a mirror of polished silver.

"How interesting!" breathed Callipygia. You don't ordinarily get a chance to see a water elemental up close, not even in Terra Magica.

She was all girl from the tummy up, with pale green skin and blue hair and eyes and very little nose. From the tummy down she was all fish, carp, the Amazon girl rather thought. Curiously enough, her body was lucent, almost transparent; she looked like something that somebody carved out of a slab of gelatin.

She also, thought Callipygia to herself rather cattily, looked blowsy and sluttish. Her makeup was put on carelessly, and she wore altogether too much for this hour of the morning. Besides that, her blue-green hair *was obviously dyed*, as you could tell from a glance at the roots, and she had rather let her weight get out of hand and could certainly stand to lose ten or eleven pounds.

Callipygia stood up and called to the water-maid.

"Hail!" she cried, waving her hand.

The Undina, who had been touching up her mascara, put down her little hand-mirror and peered this way and that in a slightly near-sighted manner.

"Yoo-hoo, up *here!*" yelled Callipygia. Putting two fingers in her mouth, the Amazon girl gave vent to a piercing whistle.

"Oh, *there* you are. I was wondering who was making all that ruckus . . . my goodness, dearie, aren't you an Amazon?"

"That I am; and you are a water elemental, I ween. However did you get here, if I may inquire?"

The Undina put her comb and mirror away and sat looking interestedly up at Cally. If Cally had never before seen a water elemental, then the water elemental had never before seen anyone like Cally. She waggled her fishtail in the water lazily.

"Oh, Gorgonzola the Enchanter conjured me up," she said carelessly. "He ordered me to infest the kingdom of Lower Pamphyllia, so that some prince or other named Florizel would not be able to go questing over in Upper Pamphyllia, where this same Gorgonzola had earlier conjured up a horrid Salamandre to vex the Upper Pamphyllians. You see, he wanted the Princess Doucelette for himself and feared that if this Florizel defeated the Salamandre and won her hand, there would be no getting her for himself . . . and, my goodness!" she gasped, "that's the longest speech I've ever made in all my life!"

"Gorgonzola, eh?" muttered Florizel, grinding his teeth. "What a caitiff rogue and varlet! Now I understand all."

"Your presence here is making the Lower Pamphyllians rather unhappy," said Callipygia, trying without very much success to be tactful and diplomatic. "Ruining their crops and all, and making everything so damp and soggy. Do you do it because you are just naturally vicious, or because you must obey your master, this rascally Enchanter?"

The Undina giggled, the giggle ending in a hiccup. She patted her lips with her fingertips.

"Beg pardon! Must have been those sardines I had for lunch. No, dearie, I make everything around me soggy and damp and miserable because it is my nature. We Undinas *like* everything around us to be soggy and damp and miserable, you see. Now get along with you before I make *you* soggy and damp and miserable."

And with that, the Undina pointed one forefinger at Callipygia's breastplate, which was of burnished steel. As if by magic, a great splotch of rust appeared upon its mirrory surface.

Callipygia was aghast; also, she was in a fury.

Florizel tugged her by one arm, coaxed her down from the crest of the hills. "Getting mad at her won't help, madam," he whispered. "Nor will trying to use your sword on her. She would just drown you in a cloudburst, or rust your sword down to a nubbin, or something."

"The hussy," growled Callipygia. Distantly, they heard the Undina's voice raised in a croon. She was singing the Bell Song from *Lakmé*, or trying to, anyway.

"We must outwit the poor, simple creature, use our superior intellect," advised Florizel. "This is one Quest where brawn and blade will accomplish nothing. . . ."

"Well, do you have an idea of how to drive the impudent creature away?" demanded Callipygia.

"Well . . . no. I'm afraid I haven't had much time to give thought to the matter—but there must be *some* way. We simply can't let this rascally Enchanter get away with his villainous schemes."

"And we can't go and fight the Salamandre so you can win the hand of the Princess Doucelette, until we get rid of this present bother, eh?" muttered Callipygia.

"Quite."

Callipygia resheathed her blade. "I suppose you're right, but the sight of that smirking hussy down there, flaunting that fishy tail of hers and taunting me with my helplessness, is almost more than flesh can bear. Maybe we can find this Enchanter and persuade him to lift the curse."

"Perhaps," said Florizel.

He sounded dubious.

It was getting dark.

9

A Royal Welcome
in Bongozinga

After a fairly comfortable night in the inn, Mandricardo and Doucelette breakfasted on bacon and eggs, toasted muffins with melted butter and fresh honey, strawberries in cream, and sizzling hot sausages, the meal washed down with steaming pots of strong hot tea.

They then proceeded by Carpet-back to Bongozinga, by which name was known the capital of Upper Pamphyllia. It was a nice little city with a white wall around it and heraldic banners fluttering from each turret top, pleasantly situated in a fertile valley well-watered by meandering rivers, and the city itself was surrounded by fields and farms, gardens and groves. Sadly, the groves were withered and the farms and gardens little more than patches of dust, so scorching was the heat in which Bongozinga sweltered. Even the rivers had dried to mere trickles.

Mandricardo landed the Magic Flying Carpet before the palace gates, and in no time at all, Doucelette was sobbing happily in the arms of her royal father, who patted her here and there about the shoulders, saying soothing things like "Now, now!" and "Tut-tut!" until she withdrew from his embrace, wiped her eyes, blew her nose with a ladylike little *honk*, and introduced him to her gallant rescuer.

King Umberto was very short and very stout, with a round face, very red, and a pair of enormous moustaches of which he was very proud.

"Very glad to make yer acquaintance, I'm sure," he said as he shook Mandricardo by the hand. "Many thanks fer rescuin' me daughter from that rascally rogue! Give yer much trouble, did he?"

Mandricardo saw no reason to come right out and admit that he had not actually engaged Gorgonzola in personal combat but had been hiding behind a stack of carpets all the while. "Surprisingly little, what," he said modestly.

"Splendid, splendid!" beamed the fat little King, rubbing his hands together briskly. "You've heard all about the fiend's cunnin' plot, I imagine. Doucey will have told yer, I'm sure."

"You mean how the caitiff rogue conjured up a bally Salamandre to plague the countryside, then promised to dispatch the vermin if you'd bestow your daughter's hand on him? Right-ho! Clever devil, what? Glad to hear you saw through his plot."

"Can't take much credit fer it," shrugged King Umberto. "Plain as the nose on the villain's face, it were. Told me guards to chase the varlet out o' here for once and all! How was *I* to know he'd do something sneaky, like kidnappin' the poor gel?"

"Couldn't have anticipated that, right-ho," murmured Mandricardo soothingly. "Still, all's well that ends well, eh? Jolly nice city you've got here, by the way."

"Call the place Bongozinga," explained the King. "Can't for the life o' me remember eggzactly why, at the moment. Not that it matters. What's in a name, *I* allers say. . . ."

"Quite," said the Tartar succinctly.

"So; hem! Just passin' through, are you, or did yer come about the Quest? Not that yer not welcome in either case," the King hastened to assure him.

"Just passing through, actually," admitted Mandricardo. "Still, while I'm here, might as well look in on this Quest you're havin'; never met a Salamandre before. Not socially, what."

"Jolly glad to have you," beamed the King. "You'll find the troublesome little beggar north o' here. Makes 'is home in the crater of an extinct volcano, 'e does. Dress light—you'll find the climate downright tropic in 'is vicinity."

"Keep that in mind," nodded Mandricardo.

Just then, Princess Doucelette came to pry him away from her royal father; she took him on a tour of the castle, and then they all sat down for a hearty lunch. So many toasts were drunk to him that Sir Mandricardo got more than a trifle tiddly on champagne, but a nice afternoon nap soon put him to rights again.

With Doucelette aboard to show him the way, Mandricardo steered the Magic Flying Carpet north of the city of Bongozinga, searching for that extinct volcano crater that King Umberto had mentioned. As they flew along, Princess Doucelette cheerily pointed out the sights to her guest.

"That's the hippodrome beneath us, and the aqueduct over there by the Pamphyllian National Theater," she was saying. "To our left you can just see the border we share with Euralia and Barodia, our neighbors—"

"Oh, I say, how jolly!" enthused Mandricardo. He remembered his tutor, when he had been a mere nipper (Mandricardo, I mean, not his tutor), teaching him all about the famous Barodo-Euralian War, fought during the reign of King Merriwig, and how the war had concluded more happily than most with the wedding of Princess Hyacinth of Euralia and the valiant Duke Coronel of Barodia.

"Romantic country, what," remarked Mandricardo. "Perfectly splendid view we have from up here."

But they had all too little time for sight-seeing, even though a Flying Carpet rather lends itself to that form of recreation; after all, they had a Salamandre to visit, and Mandricardo thought to himself that it would have been a deuced shame to have come all this long distance and to have traveled on to Tartary, without taking time out long enough to have a look at the dreaded Salamandre. After all, Salamandres don't come along every blessed day of the week, no, not in these days of the twilight of the Golden Age.

North of the capital the ground grew rough and rocky, rising into hills which buckled into cliffs and chasms and puckered into peaks. They were floating along at a moderate clip, admiring the scenery, when suddenly Doucelette pointed off to their left.

"There it is!" she said.

He followed her pointing finger: a lazy thread of smoke was coiling up against the otherwise-unblemished azure. It seemed to be wafting from a conical mountain on the horizon. Mandricardo instructed the Carpet to head in that direction.

As they neared, the temperature did indeed rise, even as King Umberto had predicted. Already a bakingly hot day, it became a broilingly hot one. In his armor, Mandricardo began to feel rather like a lamb chop on the griddle. He became red in the face; perspiration trickled down the twin points of his moustaches and in droplets from the end of his nose. He fanned himself vigorously with his helm.

"Very warm for November, what?" he murmured to the Princess.

"Certainly is," she agreed.

They brought the Carpet down to the top of a flat rock near the crest of the volcanic mountain and proceeded on foot from that point. Reaching the lip of the crater, Mandricardo peered over interestedly. He had never been atop a volcano before; they did not have such things back in Tartary. The mountains there were your regular, sensible, old-fashioned mountains: you know the kind, solid rock through and through.

Beyond the brink the ground sloped away sharply into a deep, bowl-shaped depression, all naked rock and most of it black and glittering. This was probably lava and obsidian and what-not, thought the Tartar knight to himself. At the very bottom of the bowl there lay curled up a lizard remarkably like a crocodile except that it had a three-lobed crest and was not so hard and crusty all over, as crocodiles are, nor as large.

It was cherry-red and glowing, like the end of a hot poker or a live coal. Waves of heat quivered off the creature, making its image waver like the air over a hot stove. The lava rock beneath its tummy was almost molten in the heat radiated by the lizard's body.

It was a Salamandre, all right.

Mandricardo stood up and addressed the Scourge of Upper Pamphyllia in suitably knightly terms:

"I say, what ho."

The Salamandre, which had been napping, roused itself with a start and looked about, blinking sleepily. He waved his sword and the creature saw him.

"What ho, yourself," said the Salamandre yawning again and politely patting its snout with one paw.

"A Salamandre, I take it," said Mandricardo, rather at a loss for something to say.

The glowing lizard inched about until it was facing its

interlocutor and, leaning with its elbows against the half-melted rock and cushioning its chin in both paws, looked up and regarded him amiably, tail twitching a time or two.

"And you would be a knight," said the Salamandre conversationally. "Old Gorgonzola warned me there would be knights. Not that it bothers me, for what harm can knights do? I said as much to him at the time. 'If they come at me with swords or lances or what-not, I'll just melt them down to stumps. *And* I'll broil them alive in their suits of armor.' That's what I said to Gorgonzola, you know."

"Oh; ah."

"So, if you want to come at me with a sword or lance or what-not, come ahead: it's been a boring day so far," grinned the Salamandre.

Mandricardo chewed on the ends of his moustaches and mopped his brow with a red handkerchief, then wrung it out and spread it over his armor-plated shoulder to dry. It began to sizzle slightly in the blistering heat.

"I say," he began half-heartedly. "I say . . . are you botherin' all the nice Upper Pamphyllians, what, because you like broiling them in their towns and drying up their rivers and what-not, or are you doin' it because the Wicked Enchanter makes you do it, what? Eh?"

"Oh, Gorgonzola doesn't make me do it. I do it because I *like* everything broiling hot and with dry riverbeds and all," said the Salamandre lazily. "I guess it's just my nature, is all."

"Um," said Mandricardo, gnawing on his underlip.

Then, perking up as a fairish idea occurred to him, the Tartar knight said: "I say, Salamandre . . . wouldn't you like it better in a nice dry hot desert somewhere? *You* know, with scorpions and vipers and all, where you could make it just as hot and dry as you liked and nobody would be bothered . . . eh, what?"

"Oh, it doesn't bother me if people get bothered by my making everything hot and dry," said the Salamandre rather complicatedly. "Besides," added the glowing creature after a moment, with another little yawn, "another couple of weeks more, and all of Upper Whatchumay-callum will *be* a desert, nice and hot and dry, and with scorpions and vipers and all. It's just the effect I have on places, you know. It seems to come naturally."

"Oh; er."

"Yes; now go away before your armor melts, that's a good knight. I feel another nap coming on. . . ."

And the Salamandre inched about and turned its back on him. In a few moments, a sound of gentle snoring arose form it, wafted to them on the blistering breeze.

Mandricardo went clanking off downhill to where the Carpet waited, rather feeling that he had come off a distinct second-best in the verbal exchange.

"Oh, whatever are we to *do?*" wailed Doucelette plaintively, as they flew back to Bongozinga. She was clearly distraught and was wringing her hands in helpless fashion.

"Dashed if I know," admitted the Tartar, cheerfully. The rush of air over his armor was blissfully cooling; he felt as if he had lost two or three pounds, with all the perspiring he had done back on that volcano.

"But you heard the miserable creature," moaned the Princess. "Another couple of weeks more, and all of our fair realm of Upper Pamphyllia will become a parched and desolate desert, fit only for scorpions and vipers—!"

"That's what the blighter said, all right," agreed Sir Mandricardo. "But never-you-mind, ma'm! Your royal pater and I'll put our heads together; more than one way to skin a cat, you know. Something will come up."

"Oh, but are you *sure?*"

"Never you fret," he said comfortingly. "Always dark-
est before the dawn, what. Never say die, and all that
rot. Sun never sets on the Upper Pamphyllian empire;
what I mean to say is, leave the fightin' to us men-folks,
there's a girl."

"Well, if you say so . . ." she murmured uncertainly.

"Top-hole," he said cheerfully, although inwardly he
wished he had good reason to *be* as cheerful as he
sounded. To be perfectly honest, it didn't seem to
Mandricardo as if the poor Upper Pamphyllians had a
ghost of a chance. There was no way to fight the
Salamandre so far as he could see, and no way to drive
it away. It looked to Mandricardo as if the only way to
eliminate the Salamandre from the front page of current
events would be to get some friendly enchanter to
dispose of the creature in enchanterly manner . . . and
Upper Pamphyllia seemed to be fresh out of enchanters, friendly or *un*.

Clumsily (because his steel gauntlets got in the way),
he patted Doucelette's hand, not the one wherewith
she was industriously plying her hanky and busily wiping away the tears, but the other hand that was, for the
moment, unemployed. "There, there, everything'll be
all right, what. Just you wait and see."

"I c-certainly hope you're right," sighed Doucelette.
So did he.

10

A Royal Welcome
in Zingobonga

Callipygia and Prince Florizel reached the capital city
of Lower Pamphyllia shortly before sundown. It was
named Zingobonga and it turned out to be a nice-
looking town with a regular wall around it and plenty of
turrets and towers and everything. But where the capital city of Upper Pamphyllia had been built in a valley,
the capital city of Lower Pamphyllia was built atop a
high plateau.

The Amazon girl thought that was a rather nifty way
of building a capital city. After all, from high up on the
plateau, you could see an invading army coming from
ever so far off, and have plenty of time to get all ready
for them before they were knocking on your gates, so to
speak.

She observed as much to Florizel. But the damp and
rather low-spirited knight whom she had rescued from
a watery grave was singularly unenthusiastic.

"Yes, I suppose you're right," sighed he. "Except
that when your enemy's a nasty, common sort of Undina,

there's nothing to see coming, really. Just rain, rain, rain, rain."

"Bad for the turnips, I suppose," Callipygia nodded. "Well, cheer up, Florizel; let's not worry about that now. Let's go and say hello to your royal father and find out what's for supper."

Prince Florizel's father was called King Rumberto. Unlike his royal almost-namesake, King Umberto, up in Upper Pamphyllia (who was, you will remember, short and fat and rather jolly), King Rumberto proved to be tall and thin and rather vague. He wore a long gray beard and had a monocle in his left eye, which kept popping out whenever he became agitated or got excited.

Like right now.

"An Amazon, you say? My word; how remarkable. *Amazons*—well, what next, what next?" the King said faintly, his monocle popping out like the cork from a champagne bottle and dangling, vibrating slightly, swinging to and fro from the end of its long black silk ribbon.

King Rumberto plucked it up and popped it back in his left eye. "You were rescued from the Undina by an Amazon, you say, my boy? Good gad."

"Not exactly from the Undina, sire; just from a lake. You see, she made a lake all around me."

"The Amazon did?"

"No, the Undina. And she drowned my horse—*and* my squire!" Florizel waxed downright indignant at the thought. "I can always get another ruddy horse, of course, palace stables are full of them, but where will I ever find another squire like Jacques? He certainly kept my armor burnished and oiled, and my *boots* . . . ah, me, he was a wizard with the boot-polish, Jacques was. A positive *wizard!* My boots are certainly going to miss him."

"Oh, ah?" murmured the King vaguely. Then he shook hands with Callipygia, blinking at her from wa-

tery blue eyes. "How do you do, my dear? And your
royal mother? Quite well, I hope? Don't hear much
news out of Amazonia these days, I fear."

"Oh, everything was fine there when I left," said
Cally. "Excuse me, but what's for supper?"

"I really have no idea," King Rumberto confessed.
"Something delicious, I fancy; my chef is a marvel, you
know. Well, well, so you're here about the Quest and
all, eh?"

"Well, not exactly," said Cally. "Actually, I was just
passing through—on my way east, you know," said the
Amazon girl, dodging neatly as the King's monocle
popped out again at this alarming news.

"Not that I won't be glad to discuss this problem
you're having with the Undina, that is," she added
hastily. The King, who had tottered and looked faint for
a moment, recovered his natural color and replaced his
monocle in his eye with an absent gesture.

"Splendid, splendid. Well, that rascally Enchanter
Gorgonzola, you know. A brigand, a veritable brigand."
And talking all the while, he took Callipygia by one
muscular arm and they entered the castle, with Florizel
and Blondel and Minerva bringing up the rear.

Callipygia spent a pleasant evening in the castle, basking before a roaring fire which baked the chills and
damps out of her bones and put her in a drowsy mood,
which was aided and abetted by a perfectly superb
supper—in fact, "supper" is hardly elegant enough to
be the *mot juste*. "Feast" begins to touch upon the
outer perimeters of the appropriate term.

To put it simply, the Amazon girl had wallowed in a
dinner which had begun with *Consommé aux Pommes
d'Amour* and continued from that high plateau along to
*Sylphides à la crème d'Ecrivisses, Mignonette de poulet
petit Duc,* and so on through a souffle of asparagus that

was as light as the Magic Flying Carpet, *Peche Melba*, *Mousse au Chocolat*, and assorted nuts and cheese, the whole sumptuous repast washed down with five kinds of wine and veritable buckets of dry champagne.

Toasting her toes before the fireplace, she puzzled briefly over the fact that if King Rumberto dined this luxuriously all the time, it was a mystery how he managed to remain so thin and bony. Callipygia herself had a certain tendency toward plumpness but the harsh rigors of her outdoorsy life of quests and adventures and that sort of thing kept her from actually getting, well, *fat*.

But Kings live lives of a generally sedentary nature—signing writs and proclamations and laying corner-stones and judging flower shows and giving out school prizes and so on—so Rumberto's skinniness was a real puzzler.

While his guest drowsed, deliciously full of dinner, the King busied himself discussing the Undina Situation—what else?—with some of his cabinet. The First Lord of the Snuffbox was of the opinion that it takes magic to fight magic, and suggested a prominent government official (well, say for example, himself) be sent on an embassy to tour foreign capitals, seeking to find a competent and qualified enchanter who could banish or restrain water elementals from cluttering up the landscape with their foul lakes and bogs.

But King Rumberto felt disinclined and against the notion of such junkets on general principles.

The Minister of the Royal Pincushion felt that military operations were called for in this instance. A full campaign, with cavalry and infantry and mounted archers and (why not?) a troop of elephants with javelin-throwers mounted in howdahs on their backs—surely, before such impressive forces, the Undina would wilt, turn tail, and flee back to, ah, wherever it was she had come from in the first place.

However, the King took a dim view of military operations of such magnitude, in view of the slimness of the Royal Exchequer and the estimated paucity of taxes to be gathered in this year of widespread crop failure and so on. Elephants are especially expensive, he pointed out to the minister.

Prince Florizel was still eager to pursue the Quest, and remarked that as soon as word got about to the neighboring kingdoms they would probably see a respectable turnout of knights and princes, eager for the honor of winning the Quest. Perhaps a public relations man, if one were to be retained, could mount a somewhat more spectacular advertising campaign which would make the Quest a household word for thirty kingdoms round and achieve full press coverage. You can guess by this that Florizel was of the opinion that the quicker the Undina was out of the picture and things were all fixed up here in Lower Pamphyllia, he could be on his way to Upper Pamphyllia where he hoped to get their Salamandre out of the picture just as fast, so that he could claim the hand of the Princess Doucelette.

As it turned out, King Rumberto was lukewarm on this idea, too, his feeling being that the Quest of the Salamandre would attract so many local knights and princes that there would be none left over to fight the Undina. And the reason for this was that all *he* could offer was the half of his kingdom, while up in Upper Pamphyllia King Umberto had put up the hand of his daughter, a princess of ancient lineage and remarkable beauty; also, one of eminently marriageable age.

Callipygia listened drowsily to all of these arguments, and to others put forward by the Royal Keeper of the Pocket Handkerchief, the Guardian of the Imperial Toothpick, and the Master of the Royal Shoelaces which I have not the room to go into, and thought to herself that they were all tosh.

She didn't, herself, have a good idea on how to go about ridding kingdoms of bothersome Undinas. But surely, this being Terra Magica and Terra Magica being what Terra Magica was, the problem had arisen before, somewhere. All that was needed was to look it up in a decent encyclopedia or some other reference work.

She mentioned this to Prince Florizel when, after having put forward his suggestion and seeing it rejected, he had retired, baffled and annoyed, from the fray. He thought it sounded like an excellent idea. In fact, the more he thought about it, the better he liked the notion.

"And I'll hazard I know just the book, too, Dame Callipygia," said Florizel. "Count Articiocchi's *Dictionary of Famous Quests* . . . we should have a copy or two in the castle library. I must remember to ask Signore Spinacchi about it; he's the librarian."

"Why don't you do that," nodded the Amazon girl sleepily. Whereupon she dozed off for a little, never realizing that with an impatient young lover like Florizel, to think was but to act. And it was not too many minutes later before she was rudely roused from her cozy little nap in front of the roaring fire by the Prince's hand joggling her elbow.

"I say, Dame Callipygia," he breathed excitedly, "but you were certainly right!"

"I was?" she murmured, wondering what it was that she had been right about.

"You were! I had to get Signore Spinacchi out of bed to hunt the book up for me, but it was worth it. Well, worth it to *me*, at least . . . he seemed decidedly miffed. But that's all right; he can sleep all he wants to, once the Undina's gone and everything is back to normal."

"That's nice. . . ."

"So why not let one of the footmen show you to your room and get a good night's sleep? So we can start out bright and early in the morning—as bright as it ever gets around here, that is, with all these filthy fogs and drizzle."

"Start out to do what?" demanded Callipygia, coming fully awake at this point.

"To conquer the Undina, of course. What else have we been talking about?" asked Florizel, looking surprised. "Also, by the way, we'll be destroying the Salamandre, too, which certainly makes things neat and nifty."

"You certainly seem to have been busy," observed Callipygia with a jaw-cracking yawn, climbing to her feet. "But I'm too sleepy to listen to the explanation now. You can tell me all about it in the morning."

And she went off to bed, bidding a goodnight to her royal host who, not having heard a word of what important matters had been passing between herself and Prince Florizel, was still squabbling with his courtiers over what could be done to take care of that Scourge of Lower Pamphyllia, the Undina.

BOOK THREE

Gorgonzola
the
Enchanter

11

Scorpions in Aspic

And what, you may well be asking, by this time, of
Gorgonzola the Enchanter—Gorgonzola, whose pet
Undina is rapidly turning the unfortunate kingdom of
Lower Pamphyllia into a soggy swamp—Gorgonzola,
whose pet Salamandre is rapidly turning the equally
unfortunate kingdom of Upper Pamphyllia into a desolate desert—Gongonzola, who kidnapped the Princess
Doucelette—Gorgonzola (to wind up this interminable
sentence rather neatly, I think), who is none other than
the villain of our tale?

Well, it had not taken the Wicked Enchanter very
long to discover that some miscreant unknown to him
had made off with his Magic Flying Carpet, to say
nothing of the Princess Doucelette. This quite naturally
put him in a furious temper.

As a class, evil magicians do not accept with placid
equanimity being duped, tricked, hoodwinked, or having their captive princesses and Magic Carpets snatched

from under their hands, so to speak . . . and this was *particularly true* of Gorgonzola.

His short temper and sharp tongue had already made him a leading member, in excellent standing, in the Evil Magicians' and Wicked Enchanters' Guild, of which he was a founding member. What really infuriated him was that such a large amount of good old-fashioned villainy had gone to waste in this matter. You see, just as soon as Gorgonzola had discovered from a friendly Genie of his acquaintance that the Magic Flying Carpet existed and was concealed from the knowledge of men among the stock of a third-rate carpet-monger named Yussuf Ali ben Achmed ibn Ajeeb (popularly known as "Mad Man Ajeeb" because of his bargain-rate prices on used or second-hand carpets), he had launched a cunning scheme to acquire this treasure.

Disguising himself as an itinerant carpet-monger from China, he had purchased Ajeeb's entire stock and shop as well for a princely sum, the which he paid, not in mere gold dinars, but in emeralds of the finest water. Dazzled with his sudden acquisition of wealth, Ajeeb set off for the isle of Taprobane to visit his Aunt Fatima . . . and was very much surprised, the following morning at sea, to awaken and find his hoard of emeralds had turned back into the dirty pebbles they had originally been when Gorgonzola found them.

What's the point of being an Enchanter, if you can't turn dirty pebbles into emeralds was the way Gorgonzola looked at it. And you must admit he had a point.

Then Gorgonzola posed as a lowly carpet-monger day after day while, in private, patiently unrolling or unfolding each and every carpet in his storeroom and standing on it in turn and saying "Fly, Carpet!", and getting off and trying the next one in case nothing happened. This naturally consumed a lot of his time and almost all of his patience, of which he had a remarkably small supply in the first place.

Then, having at length exhausted his patience *and* his supply of carpets at just about the same time, he finally found the one he was looking for and wasted no time at all in putting his dastardly plans into effect.

Gorgonzola, you see, was a studious and even scholarly enchanter of rather quiet habits, for a fiend, but he had this one fatal flaw which kept him from becoming a truly first-class Wicked Enchanter. That is to say, he had somehow conceived a mad and overwhelming passion for the Princess Doucelette of Upper Pamphyllia.

Why this was, no one can say. Not that Doucelette was a bad looking princess as princesses go; in fact, quite the opposite. She was a stunning beauty, with those masses of red-gold hair and those sparkling emerald-green eyes, and being such, had captivated Florizel of Lower Pamphyllia without an effort. No, the thing was, that as an enchanter Gorgonzola had his pick of the loveliest peris, the most exquisite succubi, or do I mean incubi, to say nothing of all those lady Genies who might well be delighted to make the acquaintance of a robust and healthy young Wicked Enchanter. Why, in view of all the femininity at his command, he had to lose his heart to Doucelette, who couldn't stand him for a moment, is anybody's guess.

Perhaps it was . . . *Gorgonzola's Doom.*

At any rate, his imprudent passion for the Princess blinded him to all else. He was willing, even eager, to squander a perfectly good Undina and a Salamandre of rare breeding to accomplish his villainous ends. For he knew without asking that Doucelette's father, King Umberto, would not for an instant consider him a suit-

able son-in-law. After all, who wants a Wicked Enchanter to marry into the family? Or move into the
neighborhood, if it comes down to that?

These thoughts, as it happens, were passing through
the maggoty brain of one Limburger, a pasty-faced,
pimply, weasel-eyed little lump of a man who was
Gorgonzola's servant. Gorgonzola, you see, had stomped
out of the carpet-monger's shop in a fine fury and
hastened at once to his subterranean palace, which was
built beneath the necropolis of the city. Graveyards are
favorite stomping-grounds for Wicked Enchanters such
as Gorgonzola and a perfect site to build one's subterranean palace.

So, now, picture Gorgonzola—having tossed away his
robes and turban—now pacing fretfully up and down,
muttering curses and grinding his teeth, wrapped in a
tight black gown embroidered all over with *mysterious
cabalistic signs* and girdled at his narrow waist with a
live cobra. He had no way of getting back to either
Upper or Lower Pamphyllia except the slow and mun-
dane mode of riding camelback and was trying to figure
out what to do.

Into this scene intrudes Limburger, who is setting
the table with the best silver and china and crystal, a
dewy blossom plucked from a flowering wolfsbane bush
slipped into a cut-crystal bud vase, laying out a tasty
luncheon and trying to persuade his master to calm
down and solace himself with a good meal.

"We have fresh scorpions in aspic, master—your favorite! And deadly nightshade salad and creamed toad
on toast for an *entree*, and chilled bat's brains. . . ."

Gorgonzola turned upon his little lump of a servant.
His wicked eyes were spitting red sparks from beneath
scowling black brows and his lean, sallow features were
distorted in a sneer of disgust.

"By Mahoum!" he hissed, "do you really expect me to—*eat*—at a time like this, you weasel?"

"Just a nourishing dab or two of scorpions in aspic, master. Only to fortify the inner man . . . and let me pour you a drop of this cobra venom wine . . . your favorite year," wheedled Limburger.

"By Golfarin, the Nephew of Mahoum, but I hunger only for the firm flesh and lissom limbs of the fair Doucelette," gritted Gorgonzola. "And for revenge upon the person of the nameless thief who whisked the wench from my very clutches! Not to mention my Magic Flying Carpet," he added.

"Come, now, just a spoonful, master. You must keep your strength up, you know, for your sweet revenge," Limburger coaxed. He ladled out some of the grisly scorpions embedded in quivering jelly. And despite himself, Gorgonzola was tempted . . . it *was* his favorite dish, after all . . . and he *had* missed breakfast. . . .

"Oh, by Termagant, the Mother of Mahoum, if it will make you happy, you miserable groveling wretch," he snapped, hurling himself in a chair and contemplating the table morosely. Like all of the furniture in these dank and dismal caverns, the dinner table was a ramshackle affair, knocked together loosely out of rotten boards pried from old coffins or mummy cases, or sawn from tumbledown gibbets where hanged men swung slowly in a chill, uneasy moon.

But that was not what was making him morose: far from it! Actually, such *mementi mori* as these rather tickled his fancy . . . he was, after all, a Wicked Enchanter, you must remember. No, it was the thought that here he was, wallowing in the pleasures of domesticity, enjoying a nice wholesome lunch, when even at this very moment, he could well have been soaring aloft aboard his Magic Flying Carpet, hurtling over both of the stricken, plague-tormented Pamphyllias, with a horrified Doucelette groveling at his feet, weeping in terror as he gloated smugly over her pain and his triumph . . . but instead:

"Pass that creamed toad, and be quick about it!" rasped the Wicked Enchanter as the faithful Limburger scurried to obey. Ah, by Brumagem, the Brother-in-Law of Mahoum, how the tables had been turned on the celebrated Gorgonzola!

Gorgonzola munched and crunched, gulped and swallowed, and, as often happens when a hungry man devours a wholesome and nutritious meal, somewhat of his good humor was restored by the fullness of his tummy. He began to relax. He glanced about him fondly, sipping his cobra venom wine out of his favorite goblet (it was made from the skull of a murderer strangled by his own mother), and admired the tasteful collection of stuffed infants mounted on the mantlepiece, the ornamental jar of eyeballs in alcohol on the side-table, the moldering corpse or two propped cozily in corners. Overhead, mangy, lice-ridden bats flapped and shrieked; underfoot, vipers and adders slithered over rotting bones. . . .

It wasn't much, perhaps, but to him it was . . . *home*.

"A second helping, perhaps, master?" suggested Limburger, enticingly. Gorgonzola chuckled, nodded.

"Ah, my faithful Limburger! Whatever would I do without you! When all the world turns against me," he said, crunching a mouthful of tasty bat's-brains, "when unknown enemies steal my Magic Flying Carpets, when my adored princess deserts my passionate embrace for the scrawny arms of another suitor, like that miserable little worm of a Florizel . . . at least I know my Limburger remains ever true!"

Limburger dropped fat, lashless eyelids over his squinty little eyes and simpered ghastily. For a time,

peace and quiet reigned in the noisome dripping gloom
of the black cavern beneath the gravestones, lit only by
the wan and feeble flickering of corpse-fat candles.

A fat viper slithered slowly over Gorgonzola's san-
daled foot; so relaxed and pleasant was his mood that he
didn't even crush its wedge-shaped head under his heel
as he ordinarily would have done.

Luncheon over, Gorgonzola repaired to his study and
began rummaging through decaying stacks of old books
of black magic and witchcraft, paying no attention to
the worms and spiders that ran scuttling between his
fingers as he riffled through the maggoty pages.

"There must be some quicker way of getting back to
Doucelette's side than overland by camelback," he grated
to himself, leafing rapidly through various spells, incantations, and recipes. "Travel, without one's beloved by
one's side, is such a dratted bore. How I yearn for the
day, long dreamed-of, when my Doucelette and her
darling Gorgy will be together forever, with no one to
come between them like that awful little rabbit of a
Florizel. . . ."

Suddenly, Gorgonzola stopped short and chortled with
glee. For he had found just the sort of spell he had
been looking for, an enchantment which would trans-
port him to Upper Pamphyllia and back as swift as a
wink. Eagerly, he scanned the recipe and was delighted
to discover that he already had all of the necessary
ingredients on his shelves.

Humming a little tune under his breath, he bustled
about, getting ready for the experiment.

"Let me see now, whisker of frog, ear of snake, scales
from a black cat, fingernails from an oak tree, owl's lips
. . . hmm, hmm! Mash well with mortar and pestle,
mix with sulphur and brimstone . . . let stand until it
cools, then drink. . . ."

We shall leave the Wicked Enchanter happily at work concocting one of his wicked enchantments, and return to see how our friends are faring in Upper (and Lower) Pamphyllia.

12

They Combine Forces

Mandricardo spent a comfortable night as the guest of King Umberto, and bright and early the next morning, he mounted the Magic Flying Carpet and set off to have another look at the blighter. He couldn't think of anything else to do, and, who knows, it couldn't do any harm. After all, reasoned the Tartar, the ruddy old fire elemental was an adversary you could talk to, what, and even reason with. Might be able to talk him out of laying waste to Upper Pamphyllia, what.

And Doucelette decided to go along for the ride. You would have thought that, what with having been kidnapped and carried off by a villainous enchanter, the Princess would have had quite enough of adventuring to last her for a fortnight at least, wouldn't you? You'd think she'd have felt like just lazing around the palace for a day or two, judging a flower show or laying a cornerstone or whatever it is that princesses do when they are not being carried off by villainous enchanters, but not Doucelette.

After all, getting carried off by Wicked Enchanters was more or less par for the course for princesses in magical kingdoms like this one, and Doucelette was inured to it by now.

It was a fine day, bright and sunny, with a brisk, spanking breeze. The nice weather and the excellent breakfast he had downed before setting off for a spot of derring-do had put Sir Mandricardo in a cheerful frame of mind. He felt like some small talk.

"I say; dashed fine palace your royal pater has," he remarked. "Meant to mention it last night, you know."

"I'm glad you like it," said the Princess. "We've had it ever so long. Been in the family for simply *years*."

"Noticed that bits of it looked quite old," said the knight. "Late Roman, wouldn't you say?"

The redheaded princess shrugged. "Either Late Roman or Early Byzantine. You can't always tell the difference."

Mandricardo nodded thoughtfully. Some of the Late Roman architecture had been so *very* late that it had run right over into Early Byzantine but everybody had had a good laugh at the Late Romans for being so late, and nobody minded.

As they flew on, moving ever closer to the volcano's crater in which the Salamandre was doubtless still sommnolently curled, it grew warmer and warmer. Mandricardo began to perspire in his armor and go red in the face. He began to wish he had left all those lion-skins at home wherewith his breastplate and shoulders were draped, but it was too late now.

The ground beneath their rudder (so to speak) was parched and deserty; naked stones and skulls and bones lay littered about on the burning sands, where only scarlet vipers and black scorpions slithered or scuttled, as the case may be. Here and there, a desert cactus had begun to sprout from the cinnamon-colored sands.

The Tartar looked about and spied, barely visible from their height, a lush, fertile meadow rather swampy and cool, with ponds and pools. It looked deliciously refreshing.

"I say, what's that over there? Looks dashed pleasant!"

The Princess turned her head to look. "Oh, that's Lower Pamphyllia . . . we're just about at the border. My, doesn't it look green and cool and nice," she said, fanning herself with her coronet.

Mandricardo instructed the Carpet to swerve in that direction; a little cool, moist breeze wouldn't hurt, he thought. They flew through a cloud or two, getting all dewy and damp. Dewdrops danced and sizzled on the Tartar's plate armor. he began to cool off.

"I say, *that's* better, what?" he said cheerfully.

"Very nice," she admitted. "Fly through another cloud, do!"

He steered the Carpet directly for one, but just before they reached it he seemed to spy something below them. Mandricardo uttered a Tartar war-cry—"I say! Yoicks, yoicks! Talley-ho!"—and hurtled earthward, at the swiftest speed the Magic Flying Carpet could manage, while Doucelette held on with both hands for dear life, wondering what in the world had got into the man.

Bright and early that same morning, after an excellent breakfast of crisp, succulent bacon, fluffy omelettes, and toasted muffins with honey and nine kinds of marmalade, Callipygia and Florizel saddled up and rode north to beard the Undine in her den and to set into action the plan which the young knight had devised the evening before, and which he still coyly declined to divulge to the Amazon girl.

Well . . . I say "bright and early," but actually that is not quite the *mot juste*. It was, of course, another morning of typically Undinish weather, gray and gloomy, damp and drizzly, moist and miserable. Thunder made digestive noises in the bellies of heavy clouds. Their horses picked a path between mudpuddles and the two rode with their umbrellas up, without much conversation between them, unless you count Florizel's sneezes and snifflings as "conversation." The prince had gotten rather a nasty head-cold from his experiences of yesterday.

"I do wish you'd be a dear and tell me what you plan to do," said Callipygia to Florizel.

"I cad do dad, you dow. If my blad fails, dad's dad. Bud, if id *worgs* . . ." said Florizel to Callipygia.

"I can't understand a word you are saying," said Callipygia to Florizel.

The knight blew his nose vigorously in his handkerchief, but it didn't seem to help, as his rejoinder proved.

"I cad helb id, you dow. Id's my dose . . . id's all stubbed ub."

"I'm sure it is, whatever you're talking about," sighed Callipygia. They rode on in silence from that point, a silence broken occasionally by Florizel's snifflings and snufflings and the odd sneeze now and again.

They were on higher ground now, with sopping-wet fields to either side, and, where there were no fields, plenty of bedraggled, dripping oak trees. Everything was rather boggy and sad. A wonder, thought Callipygia, that the whole kingdom doesn't expire with damp-rot.

Moodily, she rubbed a rust-spot on her armor, using a corner of her cloak, thinking all the while of the broad and sunny plains and the blue and cloudless skies of her distant homeland. Ho, for Amazonia, she thought wistfully.

Just then it seemed to get even darker. She glanced up, tilting her umbrella, and saw something decidedly peculiar. It was a cloud, of course, it must be a *cloud*, but Callipygia had never before seen one with such sharp angles and straight lines.

"Whad kind ub a gloud is *dat?*" asked Florizel bewilderedly, also staring up.

A moment later, he jumped six inches in the air—a rather difficult thing to do, when you are seated in the saddle—for his companion had let out an unexpected shriek of the sort that tends to freeze the blood. And Florizel's blood was none too warm at the moment, anyway.

No sooner had the Magic Flying Carpet settled down beside the muddy road than Mandricardo sprang from it and snatched up Callipygia—who had sprung from Blondel's saddle in the same instant—wrapped his strong arms around her and gave her such a hug that it made her ribs creak.

Built around fairly substantial lines herself, the Amazon girl sustained no damage from the embrace. Indeed, she returned it with a hug of her own that would have lamed a lover of lesser breed than the stalwart Tartar.

"By Jove, Cally! I could hardly believe my eyes— dash it all, but however did you get *here?*"

"Oh, Mandri, I was afraid that nasty Troll had destroyed you or transformed you into a stone or something!"

Talking, as the saying goes, a mile a minute, the two long-sundered lovers rapidly filled each other in on their most recent adventures, while, all the while, during the embraces and the babbling of explanations, Florizel (astride his horse) and Doucelette (atop the Carpet) looked on open-mouthed.

"I say, Cally, old girl! Sight for sore eyes, what? Who is that chap with the red nose and watery eyes you're ridin' with?"

"Sight for sore eyes yourself, and where did you get

that aerial rug, or whatever you call it, and who's the brazen hussy with all that red hair?"

Before long, explanations were finished, introductions were made, and things were sorted out rather neatly. Florizel dismounted and saluted Mandricardo courteously.

"Hail, sir dight! Blease egsguse by speege, I'b god a code, you dow."

"Not at all, dear chap, very happy to make your acquaintance, I'm sure," said Mandricardo affably. "*Gesundheit*," he added, for Florizel had just sneezed violently.

Florizel then turned to Doucelette, who eyed him coyly. He blushed violently, recognizing her instantly, and bowed low.

"Hail, brincess! I cad helb speeging lige dhis, you dow. I'b god a code."

"I quite understand, Sir Florizel," she answered sweetly. "I usually suffer terribly from them in the winter . . . have you tried hot tea with honey and lemon?"

"Not surprised the poor chap's got the sniffles, what?" remarked Mandricardo to the Amazon girl. "Deuced place is soggy as a swamp. And look at all that mist. Must be the dashed Undina these folks have been havin', what?"

"It is," Callipygia nodded. "Florizel and I were just on our way to do something about her when you came swooping overhead on that flying thing. He has this plan to rid the kingdom of the Undina, but he won't tell me what it is, except to admit that he got the whole idea from a copy of Count Articiocchi's *Dictionary of Famous Quests.*"

"Fine book, that. Never read the thing, meself."

"He says it will also rid Upper Pamphyllia of its

Salamandre at the same time, don't ask me how," she added.

Mandricardo twirled his moustaches: the dampness in the air was making them droop like day-old strands of spaghetti. "That a fact? Sort of killin' two quests with one stone, what, what? Haw!—did you hear that one, Cally? I said, 'Sort of killin' two—' "

"I heard it," she assured him.

They resolved to have a council of war on the instant, and all sat down on the Magic Flying Carpet, which was the least soggy place to sit. Florizel now held forth, as best he could, what with his awful head cold.

"Dow, here's by blan," he said. "Virst, we god do hab a liddle talg wid de Undina. We dell her whad de Salamandre's beed saying aboud her. . . ."

Florizel continued his monologue at some length, but I will not go into it at this point for two excellent reasons. For one, you are about to see the plan carried out in action, which is much more fun than just hearing an outline of it. For another, I am beginning to get about as tired of writing out Florizel's dialogue in "cold-in-the-head-talk" as you are probably tired of reading it.

So from here on at least to the end of the next chapter, I will spell Florizel's conversations as ordinarily they would be spelled, if he had *not* had a bad cold in the head. I hope you will make allowances.

And, if we are agreed on that detail, let me wind this one up so that we can get right into the next chapter and have a bit of action for a change. . . .

13

Outwitting the Monsters

They all got on the Magic Flying Carpet, leaving their steeds to roam at will in the soggy meadow and crop the lush verdure while they soared aloft, settling on the rim of the hills which overlooked the Undina's water-logged bower. They found the overweight elemental finishing up a snack of sardines.

"*Oop!* Goodness me, you popped up so quick . . . do you *have* to give a body a start like that?" she demanded, startled.

"Sorry, ma'm," said Florizel—ever the picture of knightly courtesy, even when in the company of water elementals—"but we were just wondering, my friends and I, that is. . . ."

"Well, what is it? *Hic.* There, now, I hope you're satisfied! You've given me the hiccups . . . or maybe it was that last sardine, it might have been a bit too oily. *Hic.* All your fault, I'll wager," said the Undina, crossly.

"Sorry again, ma'm, but we were wondering if you've heard any of the things the Salamandre, over in the

next kingdom, has been saying about you? I'm afraid
he's been using words like 'fat' and 'blowsy' and 'no
better than she should be' rather freely, you know!"

"Oh, is that so?" snapped the Undina, flirting her tail
dangerously. "Well, and how does *he* know what I'm
like, is what *I'd* like to know! *Hic*."

"Quite right, to be sure," murmured Florizel soothingly. "Personally, I think it's quite out of order for him
to say such things about you, really quite uncalled for.
For one thing, *I* don't think that your hair is dyed—"

"Oh!" she gasped, outraged. "And did he say that?
Hic!"

"I'm afraid so," said Florizel apolgetically, while
Mandricardo snickered into his gauntlet and strove man-
fully to keep a straight face. "In fact, worse than that,
he had been heard to observe that not only is your hair
dyed, but that the dye job was a cheap one and shows at
the roots—"

"*Ooooh!*" shrilled the Undina in scandalized tones,
flushing indigo.

"And what he had to say about your *morals* . . . well,
I'm just glad to have met you and to have seen for myself
what a fine person you seem to be, a real lady, if I'm
any judge, not the loose sort that he makes you out to
be . . . cuddling up with any cuttlefish that comes along
(his very words), and an easy mark for a shark on a lark
when it's dark. . . ."

Florizel continued in this vein for some little time,
while the Undina (and to do her justice, she was not
really very bright, but then few Undinas are, despite all
the fish they eat and which are supposed to be very
good for the brain) . . . while the Undina, as I was
saying, got madder and madder, flipping her tail and
smacking the surface of the water until she had whipped
it into a froth.

"Just you wait, Mister Knight," swore the Undina, stung to a fury by this time. She was making circular wavy motions with her hands in the air, and already a stiffish breeze was blowing up, tossing the waves to whitecaps. "Just you wait till I whip up this whirlwind, and I'll go visit Mister Bigmouth over there in that other kingdom. *Then* we'll see what he has to say!"

"'Yes, ma'm, I'm sure you'll give it to him good," smiled Florizel. "We'll be there to watch you teach him the penalty for telling tales on your neighbors."

They ducked down off the skyline, climbed aboard the Magic Flying Carpet, and went soaring over the border into Upper Pamphyllia, where they soon found the Salamandre basking in his own heat at the bottom of that volcano.

"Oh, it's you fellows again, is it?" he asked equably. "Brought some friends this time, did you? Hope you're still not trying to talk me into moving to some desert or other, because if you are, I still haven't changed my—"

"Oh, no, not at all," said Florizel. "Why, we just came from Lower Pamphyllia, and we just couldn't stay there a minute longer, what with that loudmouthed and *very* unladylike Undina, who's living over there now, you know, and the terrible things she's been saying about you. . . ."

"Oh?" said the Salalamandre, cocking his head curiously. "And what has the soggy creature been saying about me that's gotten you all upset?"

"Well, she says—mind you, sir, these are *her* words, now, and certainly not my own!—that you aren't much of a Salamandre, that your fires went out ever so long ago, and that the only way you can stay hot these days is to hang around a volcano, where it's just naturally hot."

"Oh, she says *that*, does she?" inquired the Salamandre

dangerously, slipping his forked snake's tongue in and out of his mouth very fast and looking temperish.

"She certainly does; and that's not all," added Florizel. "She went on and on about your fires being out, and said your tummy is full of cold ashes and clinkers—"

"*Clinkers*, eh?" breathed the Salamandre. Smoke and steam had begun to rise from the crater bed beneath him and his long, curved, alligatory body seemed to quake and quiver in the shimmering air.

"Yes, sir, clinkers. She says you couldn't make the water boil in a hot water bottle—that it would take two of you just to light a match—that the worst you could do to anybody would be to give them a mild sunburn if they got too close to you—"

Florizel continued in this inventive vein for a little, while the Salamandre went from a simmer to a boil. Rocks thirty feet away were beginning to blister and bubble in the heat of his fury. He started to whip his hot tail back and forth, raising dust and clouds of live steam.

"Just you wait," panted the Salamandre, "until I whip up a fire-storm . . . I'll pay the blabbermouthed lady a bit of a surprise visit, and then you'll see who can boil water—!"

"Oh, you won't have to do that, sir," murmured Florizel politely. "When we left her, she was busy raising a whirlwind to come and visit *you* . . . I believe she was yelling something about even the two Pamphyllias not being big enough for her to share with a burnt-out old fire elemental who couldn't toast a frankfurter if he tried."

"She said *that*, did she," said the Salamandre, breathing hard. "Well, just let me get this fire-storm started, and we'll see what she has to say . . . I'll show her how I can boil water!"

A cloud of sparks big as fireflies were now whirling around the furious elemental, and Florizel decided that it was time to be gone from this scene of imminent carnage.

"Sir knight, would you be so kind as to take us to the top of that mountain over there?" he asked Mandricardo. "I think it would be a lot healthier for all concerned if we were there and not here when the two elementals have their discussion. Besides, from that height we should enjoy a good view of the battle."

"Top-hole, my dear fella! Always happy to oblige. Fly, Carpet!" burbled Sir Mandricardo. He was in high good humor.

Once safely ensconced atop the nearby mountain,* the four sat down on conveniently situated boulders. The view from this height was indeed perfect, affording them a broad vista of the crater of the extinct volcano beneath their heels, and, over to the right, the green and soggy hills of Lower Pamphyllia, shrouded in drizzly veils of humid mist.

From beneath came the sound of six thousand teakettles on a boil, and a whirling cloud of sparks ascended like a meteor, for once going up instead of down.

"Here comes the Salamandre!" chirped the Tartar knight. "I say, the old fella does look mad—see the glint in his eye, Cally?"

"Positively *mur*derous!"

And, just at the same time, something like a funnel of fog appeared on the horizon, rapidly traveling closer to the scene.

"And here comes the Undina, I'll wager," smiled Florizel.

The two infuriated elementals spotted each other in the same moment and paused in their headlong flight to

---

* Its name, oddly enough, seems to have been just that. Nearby Mountain, I mean. One wonders how the cartographers know these things in advance.

circle around each other in mid-air. They did this for all the world like two prizefighters in the ring, looking for an opening in the other's guard.

"Full of clinkers and cold ashes, am I?" yelled the Salamandre.

"So my beautiful tresses are the result of a bad dye job, are they?" shrilled the Undina.

Furious, the two hurtled at each other and met in the middle.

There sounded a sound that could best be spelled *FOOMPH*, so we shall spell it that way:

FOOMPH.

The sizzling cloud of sparks vanished; so did the funnel of damp fog.

The ground shook slightly underfoot.

There rose, piling up and turning inside out and twisting and turning, a huge mushroom-headed cloud of boiling hot steam. It towered and towered and grew and grew until it was taller than the mountains.

Then it began to bend in the wind, like a top-heavy umbrella.

A stiff breeze was blowing. The upper works of the mushroom cloud began to fray and tatter, blown in the wind.

Hot as it was, the live steam quickly cooled. A pattering sounded. Raindrops were falling from the remnants of the cloud overhead. They hopped and bounced on the sizzling hot stones below.

There was no sign of either the Undina or the Salamandre. The two combatants had both vanished from view. They had destroyed each other, evidently; they had *canceled* each other.

"I seem to have missed something," confessed Callipygia. "What happened? Where *are* those two?"

"They destroyed each other, when they touched," smiled Prince Florizel. "Fire and water don't mix, you know. All that's left of them is that cloud of steam," he said, pointing to what little was left of it.

"Well, I'll be dashed!" confessed Sir Mandricardo. "Deuced clever of you, old chap, what!"

"Yes, Sir knight, a brilliant achievement," said Doucelette, giving him a coy little smile. The admiration in her emerald eyes made him turn pink and start to stammer.

"Oh, it was really n-nothing, you know," he said hastily.

"No, really," said the Amazon girl, "it really was a very clever idea. *I* should never have thought of it. Wherever did you get the idea . . . what was there in that book about quests that made you think of it? Did someone else pit a Salamandre against an Undina sometime?"

"No, not that I know of," said Florizel modestly. "But it really wasn't so much to do, you know. Not really. I mean, if you have read page 137 of the *Dictionary of Famous Quests*, the same idea would probably have occurred to you."

"Well, dash it all, sir, what *is* on page whatever-it-was of Whatzisname's book?" demanded Mandricardo.

"Oh, it's very simple," said Florizel. "You see, when the present King of Pantouflia was a young man, they were having trouble up in that country with two monsters. One of them was a remora, an ice-worm—a creature that radiates intense cold; the other was a firedrake, which radiates extreme heat. He—Prince Prigio, I mean, the present king as a youngster—taunted the two into fighting, guessing that heat would cancel out cold and, er, *vice versa*. Which is exactly what happened."

"And so, Sir Florizel, you presumed correctly that if heat and cold would cancel and destroy each other, the same thing would happen when water and fire met, is that it?" asked Doucelette.

"I'm afraid that's all there was to it," smiled Florizel.

"Good show! I say, old chap, jolly good show!" barked Mandricardo, slapping the slimmer knight on the shoulder, a buffet that might well stagger an ox. "So your quick thinking, what, has destroyed both Scourges at once, and won the Quest for you. . . ."

"And also the hand of the Princess Doucelette in marriage," grinned Callipygia.

"Hem, haw. That's right."

Doucelette turned furiously pink to the tips of her ears, and appeared to be intently studying the pebble she was shoving around with the toe of her small slipper.

Florizel, no less pink, was studying with equal intensity the shape of a cloud overhead.

And it was time for everybody to get back aboard the Magic Flying Carpet and get back to Bongozinga, or do I mean Zingobonga?

14

Gorgonzola Reconnoiters

It was sometime after these events that the Wicked Enchanter arrived in Bongozinga, flying hither on a wish, and was very much surprised and considerably displeased to find everybody acting as if they were quite happy.

He had expected to find a miserable populace clamoring for relief against the depredations of the horrible parching heat of the Salamandre and the entire kingdom slowly withering away into a veritable desert . . . but here were the cheerful Bongozingians tying up garlands of blossoms and graceful green boughs to every lamp-post and setting out long tables upon which picnic hampers were being unloaded by the wives of the happy burghers.

It was glaringly evident that some sort of public celebration was underway, although the baffled and annoyed Gorgonzola could not for the life of them imagine *what* the Upper Pamphyllians could possibly have cause to celebrate. When the innkeepers began rolling out into the town square huge barrels of ale and the town crier bawled out the news that free ale was offered to one and all, courtesy of the Palace, there no longer remained any doubt in Gorgonzola's mind.

He and his faithful henchman, Limburger, had arrived, materializing in the rooftops of the town. There they huddled among the chimneypots, peering down into the quaint and crooked little cobblestone streets with envy and curiosity. At length, the Wicked Enchanter bestirred himself and kicked his servant into attention.

"I can not bear this not knowing what is going on, by the Deggial!" he swore. "So I shall descend into the streets and seek out some responsible burgher to query on recent goings-on in the kingdom."

Limburger looked askance at this news. He eyed the lean enchanter dubiously, his beady gaze lingering on the purple robe adorned with stars and moons and comets and ringed planets, all picked out in silver embroidery, and at the live cobra which was wound about the narrow waist of his master and which served him as a belt or sash or something.

"I fear me, Master, that even the lowly peasants will know you for an Enchanter, if not in fact the celebrated Gorgonzola the Great," he began, but the other cut off his words with an abrupt gesture.

"I have already anticipated that possibility, dolt," he grated. "And I shall cast a Glamour over myself, to make it appear that I am some wealthy and powerful emir or nabob from some friendly Eastern realm, here a-visiting. That should suffice to permit me to pass among the locals without arousing their suspicions unduly."

At this happy news, the good Limburger relaxed visibly.

"In that case, dear Master, we will have nothing to fear from chance discovery," he simpered.

"My thoughts, exactly. Still and all," mused Gorgonzola, fingering his long and bony chin, "we had best steer clear of the palace. It would never do to risk running into that unknown knight who carried off my Magic Flying Carpet and who rescued the Princess Doucelette from my lustful clutches."

Limburger looked puzzled. "But, Master, why should he recognize you, when you are under a Glamour?"

"Because, fool, I begin to suspect that the Unknown possesses some powerful magic of his own! How else would he know just where and when to be in order to carry off Carpet and Princess in one fell swoop?"

"Mayhap you are right, Master, dear," said Limburger.

"Of *course* I'm right, dolt!" snapped the Wicked Enchanter. "Now, let me see," he murmured thoughtfully, "the recipe I've chosen for casting a Glamour over oneself sufficient to delude the eye of one and all requires certain ingredients which I will leave to you to procure from the apothecary shops of the town, for you require no enchantments to mingle among the populace, as you look like exactly what you are, a scurvy and skulking toady. Where is that dratted list . . . oh, here it is . . . all right, listen carefully now, we need whisker of lizard, bat's eyebrows, fish toenails, beard of jellyfish . . ." and he droned on, reading off the list until it was done.

Translating a handful of pebbles into mixed pearls, opals, and garnets, and handing these to the faithful Limburger to pocket, he waited with ill-concealed impatience while the plump little servant shinnied down a drainpipe and began hunting through the byways of Bongozinga for the necessaries. What with one thing and another, it was well into twilight before all was ready, the potion prepared and quaffed, and Gorgonzola was transformed in a twinkling into a very different sort of person, indeed.

Now he was plump, rosy-cheeked, and jolly, with the snowy beard of a patriarch and a magnificent tarboosh of green felt crusted with topaz clips, from which floated the snowy plumes of egrets. Cloth-of-gold swathed his well-upholstered form, and scarlet slippers powdered with dust of diamonds shod his feet. Limburger had taken upon himself the similitude of a towering Nubian slave with a face like polished ebony and was clad in gaudy pantaloons and red vest, holding a gold-handled parasol over his master's head.

Now suitably disguised, these two rogues descended to the streets and strolled about, observing the peasantry at their revels. On every street corner a barrel of ale had been breached and was rapidly being drained into foaming goblets, while tables bore spiced meat pastries and delectable sausages and haunches of beef dripping rich gravies and ragouts and fish stews and cauldrons of aromatic soups and cheese and pickles and . . . but words fail me.

Several thousand men and women were dancing in the streets to the music of squeaking fiddles, tootling pipes, and pattering drums. Paper lanterns wobbled and bobbled overhead, lit from within by waxen candles and shedding multicolored light. They floated like goblin moons in the skies of some fairyland, glimmering pink and yellow, white and pale blue, green and carnation through the dusk.

From time to time some stout burgher or fat-bellied merchant would hoist a tankard of ale and boom forth, " 'ealth and 'appiness to their 'ighnesses, and long may they wave!" or some similar sentiment. All of this was the cause of much mystification to the disguised magician and his accomplice.

Eventually, in one inn they paused to question a

local farmer who was well gone in his cups and who seemed to be entirely surrounded by whiskers. (Yes, it was none other than the redoubtable Tozzer himself, the little man with the bush of beard who had let Callipygia rent his rowboat so that she could rescue Sir Florizel from the lake; remember him?)

"Pray excuse me, kind sir," said Gorgonzola in suave words, "but I am a wealthy and powerful emir or nabob from a friendly Eastern realm, here a-visiting, and I confess myself somewhat puzzled by this celebration in the streets. Is it some local festival, perchance, pray tell, kind sir? Or what? And may I purchase for you another goblet of that interesting beverage you seem to be enjoying?"

Tozzer beamed fondly on the emir, or nabob.

"Why, bless yer ol' 'art, yer worship! Aren't you the generous one, now. But, no, 'tis all on 'is worship, the King o' Upper Pamphylliar, yer see. In cellybrashun o' the weddin' between 'is dotter, Princess Douceletty, and the son of 'is worship, the King o' Lower Pamphylliar, Prince Floryzel."

At this unwelcome news, the Wicked Enchanter swore a great oath by Mahoum, by Golfarin, by Termagant, *and* by Brumagem—an oath so pungent that it turned the air blue for four feet in every direction, and a distinct whiff of sulphur and brimstone could be smelled. He also ground his teeth, a particularly unnerving sound.

He opened his mouth to ask another question, but Tozzer, tossing back the last pint of ale, lazily continued. "Now, yer 'onor, as it 'appens, *I* 'ail from Lower Pamphylliar. 'Ow, then, do yer 'appen to be 'ere, me good man? you may be sayin' to yerself. An' I wouldn't be 'arf surprised if yer weren't. Because, as it 'appens, it were I what loaned me rowboat to thet gert Ammyzon lady who were the one who—"

"Amazon lady, did you say?" interjected Gorgonzola,

perking up his ears. Perhaps *this* was the Unknown whose presumed magic he feared and which fear had prompted his present caution.

"Yus," said Tozzer, accepting another mug of the blushful Hippocrene from a pink-cheeked lass who was carrying a tray laden with such through the throng of celebrants. "Hit were 'er what rescued young Floryzell from the lake, yer know. *That* were just before they met hup wif the Tartar knight, yer know."

"Wh-what Tartar knight is this? Pray tell," murmured Gorgonzola, chewing on his lower lip. The numbers of the opposition seemed to be multiplying rapidly, and he had left all of his books of magic spells, incantations, and recipes back home in his subterranean lair, amongst the spiders and the snakes.

"Sir Mandrocardy, 'e calls 'imself. Big, pow'ful-looking felly, too. Long, bright sword down to 'ere. O' course, arterwards they all went off and destroyed thet Salamandry, yer know."

"D-destroyed the Salamandre . . . ?"

"Oh, yus," nodded Tozzer casually. He reached into his thicket of beard and plucked forth a minute organism which he absently cracked beneath one horny thumbnail, flicking away the remains in a cavalier manner.

"*Thet* were the same time as when they deestroyed ther Undiny, too, yer know," he added, taking a hearty quaff from the ale mug.

Beneath his enchantment, Gorgonzola paled to a sickly hue and tottered back on his heels.

"Not the . . . the Undina, too?" he faltered. Tozzer nodded unconcernedly.

"Oh, yus! Thet's 'ow they come to 'ave a weddin', yer know. On account of the King o' Upper Pamphylliar had put hup 'is dotter's 'and in marriage to whatever Prince as whupped ther Salamandry."

"I see," muttered Gorgonzola, forcing a polite smile;

it was a rather peculiar-looking smile, most likely, because behind it the Wicked Enchanter was grinding his teeth.

"Oh, yus! So hit were thet nice Ammyzon gel as sawr thet I were hinvited to ther weddin', on account o' 'ow I lent 'er me rowboat ter rescue Prince Floryzell. . . ."

"Here, my good man, for your trouble," said Limburger, hurriedly thrusting a coin into the callused hand of Tozzer and vanishing in the throng with Gorgonzola leaning heavily on his arm.

Tozzer examined it critically. It was a gold sovereign, and stamped upon one side was the profile portrait of a bearded, slack-jawed personage wearing a sour expression ("has hif 'e 'ad just swallyed a pickle," is how Tozzer would have described it) and a crown. About the outer rim was cut the inscription CABALFLORUS. DG. CRIM TART. REX.

Tozzer hefted it. It felt heavy enough, but just to make doubly certain, he put it in his mouth and bit down. You can never be sure, he thought to himself, as he put the coin away in his pocket, satisfied as to its *bony fides*. You can never be sure with these emirs or nabobs.

The resourceful Limburger managed to procure rooms in a nearby inn for both his master and himself, despite the fact that the inn was all booked up by visitors to Bongozinga who had naturally wished to have a good view of the royal wedding procession from the rooftop of the establishment. He accomplished this by producing several more of those gold sovereigns from Crim Tartary which impressed the innkeeper no less than they had the worthy Tozzer.

Once he managed to get Gorgonzola settled down before a warm fire and had poured a carafe or two of good brandy into him, Limburger was relieved to see that the Wicked Enchanter was beginning to regain his natural color (sallow) and also to get his strength back (he gnashed his teeth together; weakly, yes, but, still, a gnashed tooth is a gnashed tooth).

The shock of learning that this mysterious Amazon lady warrior and an unknown but doubtless stalwart knight of Tartary had not only brought his beloved Doucelette together with that pudding-faced worm of a Florizel, but had also disposed of both of his dangerous elementals as if they were nothing much, had greatly unmanned Gorgonzola. This is only natural. No Wicked Enchanter enjoys it very much when his vile plots and villainies are undone by heroic valor. Sipping the brandy (it was a potent restorative, although not really to Gorgonzola's taste; he would much rather be drinking one of Limburger's cobra venom cocktails), he brooded by the fire, mourning all of his splendid wickedness gone down the drain.

". . . a good night's rest, then back home to Aegypt, eh, Master dear?" Limburger was saying.

Gorgonzola looked up, fire in his eye, one spark of which fell into the straw underfoot and started it smoldering, but Gorgonzola crushed it out absently.

"Nonsense, you dolt! I'm not going home without the luscious Doucelette in my arms and that silly Florizel of hers in his grave," grated the Wicked Enchanter.

Limburger heaved a sigh, but there was just no reasoning with his master when he got into one of these moods.

15

Gorgonzola in Disguise

The festive night ended in dawn, and the citizenry of Bongozinga, or at least those who had imbibed most heavily of spiritous beverages, greeted the rosy-fingered morn with throbbing heads, queasy tummies, and blood-shot eyes.

Gorgonzola the Enchanter could not have been in a worse humor if he *had* been suffering from a hangover which, despite the two carafes of brandy, he was not. When the faithful Limburger woke him with a pewter tray of breakfast in hand, the Wicked Enchanter indicated both his displeasure and his lack of appetite by hurling the one out of the window (that is, the tray—luckily for Limburger), and the other down the stairs.

Picking himself up and dusting off those portions of his anatomy which had come in closest contact with stairs and flooring, Limburger resolved on a more pru-dent course of action and had a huge breakfast himself while permitting his master, sulking upstairs, to recover his good humor as best he could without the assistance of nutriment.

Along toward mid-morn, however, Gorgonzola had grudgingly allowed his servant to enter the room and gloomily inquired if there was any news. There was, but none of it, Limburger feared, was calculated to bring the roses back to his master's cheeks or the sparkle to his eye.

"Let's have it, anyway, simpleton," gritted Gorgonzola.

"The newly married Prince and Princess have departed with their mysterious friends by Magic Flying Carpet for Lower Pamphyllia to visit the father of the groom and to receive the plaudits of the populace of Zingobonga," reported Limburger.

"Isn't that just dandy," snapped Gorgonzola. "Anything else, you cringing worm?"

"Yes, dear Master. The word of Prince Florizel's magnificent feat of knightly valor in conquering both the Undina and the Salamandre has spread to all of the neighboring kingdoms. Already, the honors have begun to come in. . . ."

"What honors are those, mangy cur?" demanded Gorgonzola.

"Knightly honors, Master. That is to say . . . King Prigio of Pantouflia has invested Prince Florizel with the Order of the Radish for his knightly valor, while King Giglio V bestowed upon him the Royal Paflagonian Order of the Cucumber; he also received from the King of Rubazania the Order of the Turnip and from King Alphonso of Puffleburg—"

Gorgonzola clutched at his throbbing temples with both claw-like hands. "*Enough!*" he groaned, features twisted with suffering, feeling as though his skull were about to burst—which was not beyond the realm of likelihood, considering the plenitude of royal honors wherewith his rival had so liberally been festooned.

For a long, tempting moment, the thought flashed through his tortured brain that the best thing to do would be to conjure up a couple more elementals wherewith to plague and pester the Pamphyllians, but a moment's reflection forced him to abandon this alluring idea. It is harder than one might think, conjuring up elementals and bending them to one's wicked will, and Gorgonzola just did not feel like undertaking *that* task again very soon. . . .

"M-my *head*," he moaned.

"Yes, Master, dear," said Limburger, soothingly. "Shall I fetch you a decoction of sweet syrup for your headache, or would you prefer—"

"I fear," said the Wicked Enchanter between his teeth, "that medical science has no panacea wherewith to cure the torments raging within my breast, to say nothing of my headache. No, there is but one remedy which this world affords, and that name of that is . . ."

". . . is?" prompted Limburger.

"*Revenge*," hissed Gorgonzola.

Revenge is considered by the highest authorities to be sweet; however, upon whom should he revenge his wrongs, that was the question that plagued the unhappy enchanter. That, of course, and *how*.

For it would seem that Prince Florizel and Princess Doucelette were beyond the reach of any vengeance he might manage to wreak since they were now absent from the Pamphyllias on their honeymoon (according to the Town Crier, who always dispensed the news), and precisely *where* the happy couple were honeymooning had not been divulged by the Palace. This was probably a measure intended to insure privacy for the newlyweds.

After a mediocre lunch—Limburger had managed to scare up fricasseed rats, viper's tongue in stinging-nettle salad, and a tasty snack of pickled cockroaches—Gorgonzola broodingly contemplated the courses of action open to him. It seemed to him that the punishment of Prince Florizel could wait till some future date—in fact it would have to, since there was no way of finding out where he and Doucelette were. Therefore, the most important thing to do was to recover the Magic Flying Carpet, which either Sir Mandricardo or the Amazon Callipygia, Gorgonzola still didn't know which, had stolen from him.

And while he was doing that, he might just as well turn the two of them into toads or something, he thought meanly.

The very contemplation of such villainy put the Wicked Enchanter in a better mood. He decided to visit King Umberto's palace and see what he could find out about the two strangers.

Thus it was only a little past the hour of noon when the porter at the gate announced to the First Lord of the Toothbrush, who passed it along to the Secretary of the Royal Collar Button, who mentioned it to the Hereditary Guardian of the Imperial Nailfile, who reported it to the Defender of the King's Eyeglasses—and so on and so on—that royal visitors awaited the King's pleasure.

Now, King Umberto was feeling a bit under the weather, since, if anyone is entitled to imbibe rather heavily of *strong waters* on the occasion of a royal wedding, it is certainly the father of the bride. Pushing the icebag a bit higher on his bald forehead, he peered irritably at whichever-lord-it-was who delivered the news of the visitors to him and snapped:

"Who did yer say the fellers were?"

The courtier (it was, according to the Notes in my edition of the *Chronicle Narrative*, none other than the Minister of the Royal Salt-shaker who brought the word), bowed a second time, and said:

"The gentleman did not give his name, Majesty, but

merely said he was some wealthy and powerful emir or nabob from some friendly Eastern realm, here a-visiting. And his valet."

"Um. Drat the luck! Oh, very well, Salt-shaker, better show the fellers in. What time is it?"

"A little past noon, Your Majesty."

The thought of luncheon made the fat little King wince, but the Royal House of Upper Pamphyllia was made of medium-stern stuff, and mastering the queasiness he felt at the mention of nutriment, he bade the Minister of the Royal Salt-shaker inquire of the Cook if she had any cold cuts or chicken salad or whatever to serve, and ordered that whatever she managed to rustle up should be set out in the Ninth Greater Drawing Room in the North-East Wing, to which the visiting potentate and his squire were to be ushered at once.

"When you've done that, send in the Guardian of the Royal Bath-water, the Keeper of the Brush and Comb and the Grand Vizier of the Talcum Powder. And inform me guests that I'll be along soon as I can. Tell 'em to go ahead and put on the feedbag and not wait fer me!"

Gorgonzola felt that the last thing he wanted in this world was another lunch, especially of such repulsively puerile fare, but after all, one cannot risk giving offense to one's Royal Host from whom one plans to shortly inveigle information, so, perspiring liberally, he munched away gamely on the cold cuts and chicken salad, washing the whole down with cold fresh lemonade, as the Palace Cellars were completely out of champagne after last night's banquet.

Before very long, King Umberto came hurrying into the room, his royal velvet robe with the ermine trimming on backwards and his second-best crown tipped awkwardly over his right eye. They rose and bowed.

"Greetings, sire," said Gorgonzola smoothly. "I am hight some wealthy and powerful emir or nabob from some frien—" began the Wicked Enchanter, but the King waved his hands short-temperedly.

"Yes, yes, so me Minister of the Royal Salt-shaker informed me," puffed the stout little monarch. "Very pleased to make yer acquaintance. Always happy when some wealthy and powerful emir or nabob drops in fer a chat. Too bad yer weren't able to arrive yesterday; me daughter got married to Prince Florizel of Lower Pamphyllia, yer know."

"Oh? Oh, yes," said Gorgonzola with an expression of polite interest, "I do believe they were saying something about it in the inn we passed, weren't they, Limburger, old fellow?"

"They were indeed, my lord," murmured Limburger, who was still disguised by the Glamour of Gorgonzola's spell as a towering jet-black Nubian. "Heartiest congratulations to Your Majesty on the happy occasion," he said to King Umberto.

"Thankee, thankee," puffed the King. Just then one of the footmen brought seconds on the chicken salad and set the bowl down before Gorgonzola, who groaned secretly and rolled his eyes up into his head.

Hastily averting his eyes from the sight of *all that food*, King Umberto told his visitors all about the wedding and the knightly honors granted to his new son-in-law (I forgot to mention that he, himself, had invested his new son-in-law with the Royal Upper Pamphyllian Knightly Order of the String Bean, but I can't remember *everything*, you know!), and how happy Sir Mandricardo had appeared—

"Excuse me, Your Majesty, but is that Sir Mandricardo, the son of King Agricane of Tartary?" inquired Gorgonzola in hollow tones.

"Yes it is, that's the feller," nodded the King.

"The knight-errant who helped defeat the powerful enchanter, Grumedan, and helped destroy the wicked witch, Mother Gothel, and helped baffle the Giant Thunderthighs, and helped petrify into a marble statue the celebrated Egyptian magician, Zazamanc?" asked Gorgonzola nervously.

"One and the same chap," agreed the King. "Like to meet the feller? He and his lady-love, Princess Callipygia, an Amazon gel, will be back here tonight. They flew the newlyweds over to Zingobonga on their Flyin' Carpet. Come to the Palace tonight, do; holdin' a reception fer the two o'them, and any emirs or nabobs what happen to be passin' through the kingdom is always welcome! Cook'll be servin' ragout of peacock, Bird of Paradise on toast, broiled ibis, nightingale's brains—yew feelin' all right, yer nabobship?"

The notion of more food, especially more of *that* food, had made poor Gorgonzola turn a lovely shade of olive-green, but he waved one hand feebly, pushing away the chicken salad.

"P-perfectly all right. Perhaps a bit of fresh air. Thanks for the l-lunch. Believe we will drop in on you this evening to meet the conquering hero. And heroine."

Not until the front door of the palace closed behind them did the Wicked Enchanter draw a comfortable breath.

"Do you feel all right, Master?" inquired Limburger unctuously, and rather anxiously, too.

"I've felt better," snarled Gorgonzola. "I thought that fat little fool would never stop talking about f-food . . . alas, things are far worse than even I had anticipated, Limburger!"

"Oh? In what way, Master, dear?"

"I've *heard* of this knight, Mandricardo," muttered the Enchanter. "On my last visit to the Astral Plane the denizens were full of him and his exploits, and could literally talk of little else. I was quite correct in assuming that the Unknown who carried off my intended bride, the fair Doucelette, and the Magic Flying Carpet had powerful magic at his disposal. This Mandricardo is on a first-name basis with Dame Pirouetta, the Fairy of the Fountain, with Atlantes, the Wizard of the Pyrenees, with the sorcerer Pteron of Isle Taprobane—"

"Oh, my," said Limburger faintly.

"Well might you say 'oh, my,' " groaned Gorgonzola, looking gloomy. "He is a formidable adversary, perhaps the most dangerous I have ever faced."

"Might it not be wise, Master, to eschew, in this instance, your cherished thoughts of revenge? There are, after all, other beautiful Princesses for you to carry off, and I have no doubt, other Magic Flying Carpets, as well. . . ?"

"Hmm," said Gorgonzola, looking indecisive.

Then his features hardened, and a familiar glint of stubbornness gleamed in his flinty eye. For villains of the same kidney as Gorgonzola are seldom known for acting prudently or cautiously; no, not when it comes to deferring or canceling their revenge. Still and all, this *was* the heroic and intrepid Mandricardo of Tartary they were talking about. . . .

"Well . . . we'll see," he said at length. "It will, at the very least, do us no harm to drop in at King Umberto's palace this evening and take a look at the stalwart Tartar and his Amazonian inamorata. And perhaps, while we're there, we can find out where he hides the Magic Flying Carpet when he's not riding around on it destroying my Undinas and Salamandres!"

BOOK FOUR

Akhdar
the
Green

16

To the Mountains
of the Moon

It was shortly after lunch that Sir Mandricardo and his lady-love returned to Bongozinga from their morning's visit over in Lower Pamphyllia, and when King Umberto informed them that by their absence they had missed an important visitor, the Tartar knight said "oh, ah?" vaguely.

"Yus," nodded the stout little monarch. "Seems like some wealthy an' powerful emir or nabob from some friendly Eastern realm was here a-visitin'. With his valet. Too bad you missed 'em; emir seemed quite impressed to hear you wuz around. Knew all about yer."

"Is that a fact," said Mandricardo. He had no idea who the visitor might be, and cared even less. Their interesting and valuable stay in the two Pamphyllias was, he decided, at its end; come, they had rescued two royal lovers, united them in wedlock, and destroyed two plaguesome monsters, all in one feat. Time they were moving on, thought Mandricardo.

He shared this thought with his betrothed.

"Time we were movin' on, what," he said.

"I suppose you're right," Callipygia agreed. It would be weeks before the pair of royal lovebirds returned from their honeymoon, and there was no point in hanging around the Court with nothing in particular to do. And the country of the Amazons was not too very far east of here: they could drop in on Queen Megamastaia's court, on their way to Tartary, and ask her blessing on their nuptials.

King Umberto was rather sorry to see them go. They discussed their departure in a tower room where the King had drawn his easychair up in front of the tall mullioned windows from which he happily watched the rain fall plenteously upon the parched and dessicated earth of Upper Pamphyllia, so welcome a sight after the lengthy drought forced upon them by the unwanted presence of the Salamandre.

Over in Lower Pamphyllia, they had informed him upon their return therefrom, the water-logged citizenry were basking in summery warmth. Already, a dozen or two of the lakelets caused by the Undina had dried up, the swollen rivers had reduced their foaming torrents and meekly resumed their original beds, and the fog and mist had blown away before the scorching sun, as the kingdom slowly dried out.

All was well, you might say, in the twin Pamphyllias.

"Be sorry to see yer go, young feller," sighed King Umberto. "Still and all, I know how it is! Destroy a monster here, and be itchin' to tackle another one in the next kingdom over. Oh, for the life o' a knight-errant! Well, just ask the Cook an' she'll be happy to whip yer up a tasty picnic basket ter carry on yer travels . . . unless, mebbe, yer'd like to stay around for a farewell banquet? Thet nice emir or nabob c'd get ter meetcher thet way. . . ."

"Oh, I think not, thanks awfully," said Mandricardo. "Time to be gettin' along, you know. As for this emir or nabob, don't know the felly meself. Probably just one of those autograph hunters, what?"

So they packed their gear, accepted with gratitude a bulging picnic hamper from the palace Cook, unrolled the Magic Flying Carpet, and departed forthwith for the famous country of the Amazons.

Which they were not, it seems, destined to reach. . . .

Gorgonzola spent the time pondering the problem of how to wreak a hideous vengeance upon the Tartar and the Amazon without, however, risking any reprisals from the redoubtable Mandricardo. The easiest way to accomplish such a dastardly trick, of course, would be to coax or coerce someone else into wreaking the vengeance for him, but . . . *who?* And how to persuade that someone else, however gullible?

It was a pretty problem, you will agree. But Wicked Enchanters tend to be wily and cunning, and in this respect, at least, Gorgonzola fully lived up to the reputation.

Now, as it chanced, there was among the more horrible and iniquitous of the several acquaintances of the Wicked Enchanter a certain Marid of tremendous size and prodigious strength who rejoiced in the name of Akhdar the Green, a name which was not only pleasantly euphonious but which was also not uncelebrated among the writers of fable. It was rare but not altogether uncommon, in these latter days, long subsequent to the glorious reign of King Solomon, Master of all the Genii, to encounter a member of that unpredictable and intractable species, for most of them had been shut up in magic rings or wonderful lamps or in jugs and jars, sealed with the Seal of the above-mentioned monarch and hurled into the depths of the deep green sea.

This Akhdar, however, had managed somehow to elude the common fate of so many of his kind and had resided from the days of the seventy-two pre-Adamite Sultans in certain mighty caverns situated high among the peaks of the Mountains of the Moon, as was well known to Gorgonzola, for few secrets which relate to the unpublishable histories of infamy and evil remain concealed from the diligence of the Wicked Enchanter. But, to return to our account of the famous Akhdar:

The Marid belonged to one of the most powerful of the several nations of the Genii, and had the reputation of being as short of temper as he was long of memory. And since when last they had met, Gorgonzola had tricked the rather simple-minded spirit out of a handsome set of matched smaragdines of which he had been justly proud, it was more than possible that the giant creature still nursed a grudge.

There was no point in attempting to befool the Marid by casting a Glamour over his appearance, such as he had used back in Bongozinga, Gorgonzola well knew, since Marids possess a Third Eye (situated, with admirable symmetry, in the exact center of their foreheads) which render their vision proof to such minor enchantments.

But suppose, grudge or no grudge, this Akhdar the Green should somehow become incensed against the hapless Tartar knight? Might he not then, in the fury of this more fresh and recent outrage, be willing to let bygones be bygones, and forget all about that earlier incident (now ancient history!) concerning those smar-agdines?

It was worth a try . . . and to accomplish the trick, the Wicked Enchanter decided, with a certain evil glee, to borrow a leaf out of Mandricardo's own book, for he incorrectly supposed the trick one of the Tartar's devisal. When he explained what he intended to do, his minion and accomplice Limburger looked politely skeptical.

"But, Master, is it quite safe to venture within reach of the Marid after the way you tricked him out of those jewels—?"

"Oh, by Zaqqum, toad, we must be bold and daring if we are to wreak our hideous vengeance upon this cursed Tartar and his fat-bottomed Amazon floozy!" grexed the Enchanter.

"I know, Master, but . . . ?"

"I shall infuriate the great booby in the same manner by which that vile Tartar tricked both of my elementals to their destruction," gloated Gorgonzola, rubbing his dry palms together and never minding the fiery sparks thus struck. Let them fall where they may, was his feeling.

Of course, the Wicked Enchanter errs slightly here, in presuming that the ploy by which the Undina and the Salamandre were lured into attacking each other had originated within the brain of Sir Mandricardo. But it matters little, and, after all, even Wicked Enchanters don't know everything. . . .

Ignoring the doubtful quibbles of the dubious Limburger, Gorgonzola impatiently whipped out his copper flask of wishing-mixture, uncorked it, tossed down a dollop of the stuff, gagged slighty, and wished himself atop a prominent peak amongst the Mountains of the Moon.

Instantly, he and his henchman vanished from the rooftops of Bongozinga; thereafter neither he nor his toady were ever seen again in the kingdom of Upper Pamphyllia, which was perfectly acceptable to the Upper Pamphyllians, although good King Umberto did occasionally pause to wonder whatever had become of that nice emir or nabob who had come hither a-visiting from some Eastern realm and who had so very much enjoyed the chicken salad.

In the same split-second, the two villians of our story rematerialized again, this time, as Gorgonzola had desired, atop a windswept mountain peak in the Mountains of the Moon. Fortunately for poor Limburger, who had been quite alarmed at the wording of the wish, whatever Genie it is who receives and obeys magical wishes somehow knew that the Wicked Enchanter meant, not the alpine heights of our neighboring world in space, but a certain range in the northwestern parts of Afric, not far from the burning and trackless sands of the ill-rumored Moghrab.

"Splendid, splendid!" hissed Gorgonzola, grinning a particularly nasty grin and showing that all of the teeth in his head *had been filed to sharp points*. "By the Zamzam," he added, "the potion works excellently. I had my doubts about the freshness of those bat's whiskers. . . ."

Limburger looked about, pulling his dirty robe more closely about his chilled shanks, for the wind was sharp and cold at this height. The vista that met his gaze was not exactly one calculated to restore his good humor. Under a sunset sky of sulphurous yellow, turgid with seething masses of ominously dark storm-clouds, which roiled and rumbled, their bellies filled with undigested thunders, lay a stark wilderness of naked rock, cloven by monstrous convulsions of nature into horrible ravines and shattered peaks. He and his master stood upon the very brink of a vertiginous abyss; far beneath their heels, a leaden rivulet of poisonous alkali crawled sluggishly.

Nowhere within the reach of the human eye could be discerned a single living creature, even for the lowliest species. Not a squirming reptile, a slithering scorpion, a venomous clump of cacti—not even, for that matter, a single blade of humble grass. Indeed, this terrific vista of claw-like peaks and horrible chasms, all hideously bathed in lurid light, might well have been part of the very mountains of the Moon, for all the life that Limburger could observe.

He shivered slightly; but, however little his pudgy and pasty-faced henchman enjoyed the wilderness of tortured and tumbled rock, Gorgonzola reveled in it. A Wicked Enchanter to the core, such landscapes of hideous desolation delighted him, and soothed his perturbed spirit much as a gentle and dewy garden close might sooth you or me.

Tucking away beneath his robes the coppery flask of wishing potion, Gorgonzola set about locating the cave wherein dwelt the Marid. Since the wish had deposited them upon this particular peak, it was obvious to him that the Marid's cave could not be far removed, nor, indeed, was it, as was soon proved. He clutched his crony by the upper arm, hissed "*There!*" and pointed to their left, where one could easily perceive a black and horrible opening, doubtless the mouth of a monstrous cave.

They entered, stumbling into stalagmites, or do I mean stalactites? I never can remember which ones dangle from the ceiling and which ones stick up from the floor of a cave, unless I look them up in the dictionary. Anyway, they blundered along, running into the stony spears, tripping over the skulls of monsters, stepping into puddles of reeking slime, until they turned a corner and, lo! the cavern opened out into a scene of such stupendous magnificence that I am going to save it for the next chapter, rather than try to cram it into this one.*

* I was right after all: it is stalagmites that are the ones that stick up from the floor of caves! (I looked them up in the dictionary.)

17

The Three Temptations

At the spectacle which met their astounded eyes when
they had turned the corner and were about to enter a
new and even more vast cavern, both the Wicked Enchanter and his henchman stopped short, and I would
be shirking my duties as a chronicler if I did not
admit that a gasp of astonishment was wrung from their
lips.

They stared about in amazement at finding themselves in a place which, though roofed with a ragged
ceiling of naked rock, was so spacious and lofty that at
first they mistook it for an immeasurable plain. Their
gaze discovered rows of columns and stately arcades
which gradually diminished in the distance until they
terminated in a point. Beneath their heels lay a pave-
ment strewn with gold dust and saffron, from which
emanated an odor so subtle and delicious that it almost
overpowered their senses, to which were superadded
the fumes which coiled into the air from immense cen-
sers of pierced bronze and wrought silver filigree, which

contained glowing coals upon which lumps of ambergris and the shavings of the wood of aloes were burning.

Between the columns (which were of malachite, lapis lazuli, onyx, and prodigious shafts of ivory hewn, you might presume from their size, from the very tusks of the Leviathan) were spread tables, each laden with a profusion of viands and wines of every vintage from the excellent white wine of Kismische to the superb red wines of Schiraz. There were whole roast boars recumbent on brass platters and smoking from every pore; peacocks, stuffed and roasted, with all their feathers replaced in their savory carcasses; succulent ragouts of lamb and aromatic kebabs of beef and green peppers; soups of every description steamed fragrantly in tureens of beaten gold; pyramids of fresh fruit—oranges, limes, pomegranates, apples, kumquats, guavas—resting on beds of fresh snow; a prodigiousness of smoking pastries, a profusion of candies and jellies, a plenitude of sweetmeats.

Limburger, reacting to this sumptuous feast, was about to fall upon it as one famished, but his master restrained him curtly. "Touch neither crumb or drop nor morsel of this repast upon very peril of your life!" the Enchanter admonished his servant. "Know, fool, that this is but an entrapment of the cunning of the Marid, who condemns to an eternity of cruel servitude the unhappy traveler or thief who mistakenly helps himself to this tempting array of delicate viands. Let us proceed further into the cavern."

Shuddering at the realization that he had almost succumbed to the lethal temptation, Limburger scurried at the heels of his master. They passed through a hanging of rich lace which veiled a graceful portal.

They passed from the Hall of Viands into a dim, rosy-lit chamber whose curved walls of luminous nacre resembled the interior of some prodigious pearl. Here were strewn soft couches and pillowed ottomans upon which reclined an infinity of desirable women, the daughters of every race under the sun and of every age from nubility to sumptuous matronhood. The nostrils of the Enchanter flared lustfully and his servant gaped ludicrously as they glanced about.

To every side sprawled nude women of astounding beauty and incredible variety. There were Negresses like languid panthers, their sinuous limbs, oiled with nard and amber, agleam in the rosy light like waxed ebony; Georgians with tumbling ringlets of purest gold and white limbs like living alabaster; luxurious Jewesses with opulent bosoms and curling red manes; slim, exquisite yellow maidens from the Isles of India and China, with piquant almond eyes which peered curiously and invitingly at them from under huge masses of ink-black hair elaborated into fantastic structures and pinned with thin blades of bamboo and jade and carnelian.

Surely the harem of no emperor since the redoubtable Solomon himself had housed such a various horde of femininity! And from lips plum-purple, scarlet, palest pink fell in liquid syllables alluring and beckoning phrases, as woman after woman invited the two intruders to pause in their progress, to rest and refresh themselves, and to partake of the pleasures of their couch. It would have taxed the austerity of a thrice-devout hermit to resist such honeyed blandishments, and, indeed, the sorely tempted Limburger, his blood heated by gazing upon such curvaceous expanses of naked flesh, had already stretched forth a hungry hand to fondle the nearest succulent thigh, when the Enchanter sternly bade him resist this temptation as he had that of the feast that had been spread before them in the outer precincts.

"To so much as stroke a lock of the heads of these

ladies, or to prod a ripe breast, is to instantly consign
yourself to a doom everlasting and horrible," predicted
the Enchanter in gloomy tones. "For this is but another
temptation which the cunning of the Marid has set
like a trap athwart the path to his throne. Come, let us
proceed."

And averting their eyes from so much bared beauty,
the two hastened through the enormous boudoir and,
drawing asunder a hanging of lion-skins stitched together with silver wire, passed into the chamber that
lay beyond, where an even greater temptation awaited
the intrepid adventurer.

Here the shaken Limburger cried aloud and all but
fell upon his knees, for great urns and casques lay
thick-set to every side, and within each blazed and
glittered a profusion of gems beyond the most perfervid
dreams of Croesus.

There were alexandrines like split droplets of purple
wine, topazes like the eyes of panthers, tourmalines
like the flesh of ripe melons, emeralds green as lagoons,
amethysts like shards of deepest sunset, opals whose
ever-mutable hues ravished the entire spectrum. Greatly
tempted, Limburger stretched forth one hungry hand
whose trembling fingers lusted to scoop up a satrap's
ransom and pour it into his purse, but the burning and
contemptuous gaze of Gorgonzola held an unspoken
warning.

They passed on, to where rubies pulsed like live
coals, and pearls were strewn like miniature moons,
and zircons glittered like sharp ice-crystals, and lumps
of amber held frozen in their smoky depths fantastic
insects and bizarre reptiles, and sapphires sparkled like
bits of twilight skies, and carbuncles gleamed con-
densed from the urine of lynxes. And again the greedy
Limburger, unbearably tempted, would have buried

both hands to the wrists in the glittering treasure, but for the stern reproof of Gorgonzola.

Passing further into the Cavern of Gems, they gazed upon garnets like clots of blood, great diamonds like stars fallen from the night skies, beads of jet like bits of polished darkness, sunstones of honey-hearted fire, chunks of turquoise like pieces of morning, fragments of rose-crystal beyond price, and stranger and even rarer gems of every color and description to which the travelers could put no name, for each was unique and one of a kind, having been prized from stones fallen from the moon.

This last temptation was the one which wrung Limburger, at least, the most severely: one handful, at the very most, *two*, and the plump and pasty servitor could have enjoyed the rest of his days in luxurious ease, with servitors of his own to wait upon his most idle whim. But needless to say, to have snatched up the smallest gem from the Marid's trove would mean to fasten the fetters of thralldom about one's own wrists for eternity.

The two emerged at length, sorely tried and inwardly shaken, into a vast rotunda which was the hub or nexus of elaborate perspectives of halls and galleries and arcades, which receded on every side into the distance, and which were all illuminated by the lurid flames of torches and braziers whose flames glimmered in long lanes the length of each vault or gallery, and each doubtless tended by the invisible hands of spirits sworn in servitude to the mighty Djinn.

In time the two came to a place where long curtains brocaded with crimson and with gold fell from all parts in striking confusion. Passing through this blaze of drapery they found themselves entering a vast tabernacle carpeted with the skins of tigers and of leopards. And here, at Gorgonzola's insistence, they prostrated themselves before the ascent to a lofty eminence whereupon whirled a globe of fire; and throned upon this globe as upon some burning throne was a titanic figure which could only be that of the powerful Marid whose dominion this gigantic congeries of halls and galleries represented.

At his first glimpse of the Marid, Limburger turned as pale as parchment and all but fainted dead away, so hideous was his visage and so malign and threatening his demeanor. This Akhdar was, it seems, most aptly named, for his hide was as green as verdigris, and three eyes of scarlet fire blazed under scowling and beetling brows, the third being situated slightly above and between them. His beard was thick and shaggy, each strand thereof as thick as a viper, and great curling tusks gleamed through the forest darkness of his terrible beard. His brows were adorned with heavy horns like antlers, many-branching, and from the pendulous lobes of his ears hung polished human skulls, while threaded upon a thong, the right hands of apostate kings and coward knights hung about his massive throat.

Twenty times taller than a man was Akhdar, throned upon a gigantic chair hewn from black gneiss studded with carbuncles blue as fire, and in his right hand he clenched an iron club longer than a canoe, set with a bristle of terrible spikes.

His triple gaze brooded down on them as they groveled, and when he spoke his tones were not unlike the sound of distant thunder.

"Well, manlings, you have passed at your peril through the Three Temptations which are set as traps before my Seat, and I observe somewhat to my surprise that to none of the three have either of you succumbed, although I have always understood that the flesh of mortal men is frail and lustful and rarely unable to resist the temptation of its appetites. Natheless, I am bound by the law of Getiafrose (whose breasts are like the rosy domes of Shadukiam) to hearken to the words of whosoever passeth the Three Temptations unscathed, withouten ripping them asunder into quivering fobbets of dribbling gore, the which I am powerfully inclined to do. So speak, by Kashkash, and to the very point, for my patience is scant, and one of you at least is an individual with whom I mightily desire brief private converse concerning the matter of certain smaragdines. . . ."

The sound of distant thunder that was the Marid's voice died into shuddering echoes, and Gorgonzola rose to his feet and made a profound *salaam*, and began to speak as follows.

18

Snatched!

The Tartar knight and his Amazonian lady-love departed by Magic Flying Carpet from the capital city of Upper Pamphyllia as scheduled and flew due east and just a trifle north. Obligingly, the Carpet expanded its dusty and threadbare self to a size sufficient to accommodate its two riders and their steeds.

It was Callipygia's task to soothe and quiet the horses and the mule, the mule in particular, for plump little Minerva became rather restive when they flew through low-flying clouds. The two war-horses, while they probably liked the experiences as little as did Minerva, had, after all, their dignity to maintain in the teeth of adversity.

On the whole, they were as well-behaved as any two war-horses could have been, when expected to travel through the skies on a flying bit of floor-covering. I wonder if my reader or myself would have faced the novel experience with the same modicum of casual aplomb.*

---

* I doubt if I could, but for all I know, you may well be made of sterner stuff. My readers tend to be a hardy breed.

They were making excellent time. The morning was clear and cloudless, and they had a brisk, spanking tailwind which helped to carry them along. They flew over the southern parts of the kingdom of Paflagonia, followed by the northern parts of the kingdom of Aphania, where Queen Petsetilla reigned with her Prince-Consort, Remsky. Then they flew over Crim Tartary, a country which had gone not-unrecorded in song and story; they passed, in point of fact, over the very battlefield where-upon the historic Battle of Rimbombamento was fought, whereon the famous Prince Bulbo, son of the usurping Duke Padella, defeated ten thousand giants and their dread potentate, the King of Ograria.

But these matters belonged to history and they con-sidered them but idly, as they laughed and chatted, happy to have resumed their journey and to be on the way to Tartary.

"I say, you should have seen my face, m'dear, when I vanished in that Troll's cave, only to pop up knee-deep in the bally sands of Aegypt," chuckled Mandricardo.

"Well, you should have seen *mine*, when I saw you vanish!" grinned Callipygia. "I didn't know what was happening. First I thought you had been destroyed, then I figured you had probably been turned into a toadstool . . . or even a toad!"

He grinned, twisting up the ends of his droopy black moustache; Mandricardo was in rare good humor.

"You pro'ly thought it was the Troll, gettin' back at us for borrowing its nice, snug, warm cave and leavin' the poor old blighter outdoors on a snowy night," he chuckled.

Callipygia agreed that such had been her supposi-tion. "But it couldn't have been the Troll," she rea-soned, "although I suppose Trolls can have magic as well as anybody. Because the next thing that happened to me that was magical was a *good* thing. So it couldn't have been the Troll. . . ."

She had told him earlier how she had been stymied of a means to cross the abyss the day after he had so mysteriously vanished from the Troll's cave, and how some unknown magic force had whisked her a thousand miles away, plunking her down on a muddy road between two water-logged meadows in Lower Pamphyllia.

"Wonder if we'll ever know what it was all about, eh, old girl?" he mused. Clear, sunny days sometimes put Mandricardo into deeply philosophical moods, like right now, as he pondered the Unknowable.

Except that the day was no longer clear and sunny. Not at all. In fact, a dense black shadow had fallen across the Carpet, plunging them in blackest gloom, and a brisk and oddly *rhythmic* breeze had sprung up from somewhere and was riffling the tasseled fringe of the Carpet.

In the next moment, Callipygia looked up to see what sort of a cloud had eclipsed the sun.

And in the very next moment, she threw back her head and screamed shrilly!

But it was by then too late for screams to do anybody any good, as Mandricardo would have been forced to agree. For, just then, he found himself upside down, standing on his head, jammed in between Bayardetto and Blondel, with the Carpet closed about him like a tent which had collapsed. He couldn't see, he couldn't move, and it was all he could do to yell, and when he did, no one could have heard it over the frightening neighing of the two horses, or the screaming of Callipygia, or the braying of the little mule, or . . .

. . . *Or the thunder of mighty wings!*

Gorgonzola had seldom waxed as eloquent as he waxed then and there before the fiery throne of the Marid.

With all his wily eloquence, the honey-tongued Enchanter played upon the emotions of the cunning but rather simple Genie. According to Gorgonzola, the infamous Mandricardo had blackened the good name of Akhdar before the nations and had tarnished his reputation among the Genii.

"But why, O Enchanter, should this Tartar knight so curse and defame me, who have never ere this given him cause to be mine foe?" inquired the angry Marid, beating his great black wings together like claps of thunder and breathing fiery sulphur and brimstone. "In the name of Kashkash—*why?*"

That was an excellent question; it was, also, an eminently predictable one, and, in preparation for this moment, the Wicked Enchanter had taken the time to think out some good (if spurious) reasons.

"Overweening pride, O mighty Akhdar!" the Enchanter declared in ringing tones. "Having destroyed or at least discomforted ere this not only a Witch and a Wizard, a Giant and an Efreet," he said, grandly skipping over the leading role which Mandricardo's friend and companion, Sir Kesrick of Dragonrouge, had played in the above-mentioned destroyings and discomfitures, "there now remains no more dreadful adversary yet to be whelmed beneath his valor but a very prince and potentate of the famous tribe of the Marids! And what more redoubtable a Marid could be mentioned on the lips of men than that of—*Akhdar!*"

"There is, of course, something in what you say," grinned the Marid without a shred of modesty. His grin was fatuous, and with one horrendous claw he preened the matted and filthy feathers which adorned his monstrous vulture-wings.

"And so he names you dastard and villain, not to mention caitiff rogue," continued Gorgonzola glibly. "It is the lying claim of this vagabond of a Tartar that you hide here in your comfortable cave, while he rides the wide world issuing his boasting challenge to you to show yourself and face him in honorable combat."

"I will crush him underfoot as a gardener crushes the unworthy snail," growled the incensed Marid, gnashing his tusks ferociously, with a horrible rasping sound that made Limburger's stomach heave queasily, and also made the little man glad that he had not paused to revictual himself at the Genie's tables in the forecourt.

"I'm sure you will," hissed the Wicked Enchanter pleasantly. "And when you do, a favor—a trifle, nothing more. There will be a faded bit of carpet about his person, which I would like as a souvenir of your victory. 'Tis but a little thing to ask!"

"It shall be yours," rumbled the Marid.

"If, that is, you know where the boastful braggart happens to be," continued the Enchanter anxiously. "For all I know, he may have left Upper Pamphyllia already, continuing on his way, spreading defamations on your character and name far and near."

The scowling brows of Akhdar blackened, and his eyes, rolling with fury, resembled red-hot meteors. The third eye in the middle of his forehead now opened, it having been half-shut in a drowsy nap, and by its supernatural mode of vision the Marid was able to locate Mandricardo in an instant.

"He has, O Enchanter, and even at this moment flieth over the kingdom of Crim Tartary, whither I am bound upon the instant! It will take my powerful wings no great time to bear me to his side, and then the world shall bear witness as to whether or not the brave Akhdar ever blenched from battle!"

Gorgonzola drew the copper flask from beneath his robe and took a swig of its sorcerous contents.

"I will be there before you, O Akhdar," he promised, as the giant pointed his massive iron mace at the rocky ceiling far above their heads. Thunder rolled; lightning flashed, blue as the flame of acetylene. The rocky dome cracked asunder and split, revealing a glimpse of the lurid and sanguine glow of sunset skies. Through this opening the gigantic and terrible Marid flew on whirling pinions.

"Remember, don't forget about the carpet!" Gorgonzola called after the huge creature as he rapidly dwindled in the distance.

With dawn, the mother Roc had left her nest and the hungry, squalling brood of baby chicks it contained atop the snow-clad peak of Mount Caucasus, and soared aloft, hunting for the wherewithal to feed her hatchlings.

Immense beyond thought was she, a veritable Behemoth or Leviathan of the skies, her feathers bronze, copper, gold, the great wingtip-feathers blood-scarlet, as was her knurled crest or topknot, her beak and claws beaten gold.

She flew first across the Roof of the World to the seas which lay beyond China, in whose midst swam the mysterious, seldom-visited isles of Zipangu. Here she kept sharp watch—with eyes a thousand times more keen than those of hawk or eagle—for the Great Sea Serpent which betimes haunts these lonely Eastern waves.

Then she flew north to the utmost shores of the world, where the icy black waters of the Frozen Sea lash in their primal fury the rock-bound coasts of Hyperborea, Cimmeria, and Scythia. Floating aloft like some titanic and monstrous cloud, she searched with keen gaze the stormy waters, which were oft, as she knew from old, the chilly haunts of the enormous Rosmarin which were wont to bask upon the gritty shores or ride the ice cakes spawned from mighty glaciers.

Again her quarry eluded her searching gaze, so the great Roc turned her flight westward and soared aloft out over the measureless leagues of Mare Tenebrosum, the Sea of Darkness*, in search of the mighty whale.

Turning at length from her fruitless search, the Roc flew across the world. True, Oliphants and the huge, lumbering Monoceros were smallish game for her famished and greedy brood, but they were known to haunt the plains and jungles of Hindoostan, so she wended her way thither, pausing, albeit briefly, over the thick forests of the Rhineland, to eye speculatively a sizable Ogre. He was a particularly fine specimen, fat and juicy, but the Roc little liked the look of the great spiked club he bore on one hairy shoulder. And Ogres, she knew, *sometimes bite*.

It was not until she hovered, vast wings enshadowing the world, floating on the calm skies above Crim Tartary, that she spied far beneath her a moving shape that seemed large enough to afford sufficient nutritive value to assuage the hunger of her hatchlings.

True, she could not at a glance identify the flying creature, whose singular shape—squarish or rectangular—and whose unlikely hue—faded scarlet, with minute markings of green, indigo, yellow—resembled no form of aerial life large enough for her to be familiar with. But, whatever it was, it should serve to feed her young, and the day was wearing on. So, folding those enormous wings that enshadowed an eighth of a continent, she plummeted from her great height, spreading her vans in the last moment to break her fall, as

---

* In Terra Cognita, this is known as the Atlantic.

her outspread claws snatched the flying thing from the skies.

Then, bearing the Magic Flying Carpet and its contents like a snack wrapped in a handkerchief, she flew home to her nest atop Mount Caucasus.

19

Out of the Roc's Nest

Arriving at Mount Caucasus, the mother Roc hovered
on throbbing vans above its snowy crest, aimed, and—
dropped her burden!

Within the folded carpet, jammed head-down between two sweating and very frightened horses, Mandricardo was in total darkness and helpless to extricate
himself from his predicament. The worst thing, of course,
was that he hadn't the faintest idea of what was going
on.

When they hit the nest, he went *oof!* and saw stars
(being head-down, you remember). Then, there was a
rift in the gloom, and blessed daylight peeped through.
It was Callipygia, atop the heap, standing, or kneeling,
actually, atop Minerva's belly while she threw open the
folds of carpet.

She took a long look around, then dove back in and
tried to help Mandricardo. She laid hold of his boots
and tugged and tugged. Before long, he came clear of
the press like a cork out of a bottle—purple in the face,

soaked with sweat, his helmet askew, hair in his eyes, swearing by half the denizens of this or that heaven, or, at the moment, hell.

"—By Loki's lower lip! by the adams'-apple of Angra-Mainyu! By Nergal's nostrils!" he raved. She shooshed and shushed, eventually getting him set rightside-up and somewhat calmed down.

"What happened, dash it all!" he demanded hotly. "Bally Carpet just folded up in midair—the *horses*—!"

Having swiftly considered the evidence immediately to hand, Callipygia had arrived at a few answers.

"I think we were seized in the claws of a Roc," she said. It had a certain calming effect upon the Tartar knight. Even, you might say, an unnerving one. After all, you don't fool around with creatures to whom elephants are the size of guinea pigs.

"Good gad," blurted Mandricardo, goggling. "A bally *Roc*, you say . . . but where did the blighter get to?" Peering around, he saw only the peaks of nearby mountains, misty valley beneath these, and the steely glint of a distant sea.

"Flew away," said the Amazon girl grimly, "leaving us here to serve as luncheon, stuck atop this mountain. We're in a Roc's nest, Mandricardo. Take a look for yourself."

It not being the sort of thing you'd care to take someone else's word for, he did. They were sitting in a tangle of carpet amidst a gigantic nest of knitted treetrunks and branches. Scattered feathers were woven into the intertwined trees, and these were as big as the leaves of a palmtree.

"Seems to be a Roc's nest," the knight admitted.

Callipygia pointed.

"And there are the Rocs," she said bitterly. "It would seem that we were brought here as lunch for the goslings. Roclings. Whatever. . . ."

"Rocettes?" mused Mandricardo. Not that it mattered. They were bigger than bullocks and many times uglier. You know how ugly newborn ducks are, scrawny, patched about with fluff, all straining wattled necks and wide-open, gaping beaks and hungry eyes. Precisely! Now imagine those grown to the size of water buffaloes, and you will have some notion of the unwelcome creatures wherewith the Roc's nest was adorned.

There were six of them, and they looked ravenous. Cawing like a hundred gulls, the ugly and ungainly creatures waddled and flopped toward the fallen Carpet, which lay in one corner of the nest. The bottom of the nest, incidentally, was littered with odd, angular-shaped slabs of some hard, milk-white ceramic, as it seemed. They were either concave or convex and about thirteen inches thick.

It took a little imagination to realize that what they were was *eggshells*. Or parts of them, anyway; it would seem that the baby chicks had only very recently emerged to the light of day.

Mandricardo tightened his jaw muscles and drew his shining sword. It is rather unsettling to discover yourself considered as a lunchtime snack by something the size of a water buffalo . . . *dash it all, and it was such a nice day, too,* groused Mandricardo to himself. Well, at least he and the Amazon girl were still armed and could, no doubt, give an excellent accounting of themselves.

He said as much to the girl. She agreed, but in her sometimes annoying and very practical manner pointed out that this would not exactly endear them to the mother Roc when she returned to the nest to enjoy her own lunch, whatever it might be.

Mandricardo had not thought of this possibility. It was true, swords or no swords, they could hardly fight anything as big as a full-grown and very upset Roc.

Mandricardo peered about, trying to think of a way out of their dilemma. To every side, the mountain sheared off into vertiginous depths of emptiness. Trying to climb down from such a height would truly be a feat, especially since they had the horses to consider. Not to mention Minerva the little mule. And it *did* seem a shame to have to use sharp steel against these awkward, almost helpless, and remarkably ugly little monsters. Both Mandricardo and Callipygia felt the same squeamishness at the thought of having to slaughter them.

In the next instant, the Tartar smote his brow with the palm of his hand, grinning with relief.

"I say, Cally! We'll simply fly out of here on the dashed Carpet. We don't have to kill the chicks at all—"

"Then we'd better get going, because they're almost upon us," she said between her teeth. Flopping and floundering, the baby Rocs had almost reached the Carpet. The fact that their mother had built them a nest the size of the Rose Bowl (not that the simile would have occurred to either our hero or our heroine, of course), is all that had kept them from reaching the two man-sized tidbits long before this.

"I say, Fly, Carpet!" bawled Mandricardo, as the first Rocette made a snap at his head. In the next instant, the world tilted and fell away at a steep angle. Falling prone and clutching at the ragged fringe of the Carpet, the Tartar squeezed shut eyes watering in the wind, took a look at the dim valley swinging up at his face with sickening speed, uttered a strangled gasp, and shut his eyes entirely. Nor did he open them again until the Carpet had settled quietly to earth some distance away from the foothills of Mount Caucasus.

When this had been done, he pried open his lids, let go of the fringe, sat up, said *whoosh!*, and grinned shamefacedly at his betrothed.

She was in no better shape than he was and slightly green around the gills, as the saying goes. The Carpet's steep descent down the side of Mount Caucasus had been as unsettling as a ride on a toboggan.

They led the horses and the mule into the field which lay before them and quieted the beasts. Erelong they were calmly cropping the lush grass, which made Mandricardo subtly aware of a void in his own midsection. And Callipygia was as hungry as he; unfortunately for their picnic hamper, the cooking down in Lower Pamphyllia had rather spoiled the Amazon girl for roughing it. When they could have been sitting down to *Timbale de ris de veau Toulousiane* or *Selle d'Agneau aux laitues à la Grecque* at King Rumberto's table, they didn't exactly get excited at the thought of potato salad, hard-boiled eggs, and cold cuts.

"You scout around for some fresh water, while I see what game I can find," suggested Callipygia. "I feel hungry enough for a hot meal."

And, taking up her bow and quiver, the Amazon stalked off toward some distant trees.

"Right-ho!" said Mandricardo agreeably. He looked about and was lucky enough to spy what could only be a well of stone atop a nearby hill, and headed for it, leaving the livestock to continue filling their bellies.

The hill had three sides that were steep and sheer walls of rock, but the fourth side afforded easy access to the well on its crest—if "easy" is quite the *mot juste* for a road guarded by six incredible monsters! Mandricardo stopped short and stared. He also admitted that he was dashed.

The cause for his discomfiture was simply explained. The road (path, rather) curved between five posts of verdigris-eaten bronze. To each of these there was tethered by a strong chain of the same metal a beast noted

in fable and featured, it may well be, in the more
learned of the bestiaries.

Mandricardo had enjoyed the usual education afforded
to princes, which is to say that beyond being able to
con his letters and conjugate Greek, his learning was
limited to the equestrian skills, hawking, swordplay,
hunting, Court manners and protocol, heraldry, and
the composing of sonnets to his mistress' eyelashes.

However, even Mandricardo could recognize *these*
monsters, for each of them was utterly unique. These
one-of-a-kind brutes made up a collection that would
have brightened the private menagerie of any powerful
sorcerer—such personages being rather given, as Mandricardo had always understood, for one reason or another, to the compiling of such private zoos of fabulous
beasts.

There was no mistaking the Bleps—it was the black
Bleps, of course, and none other—or the Strycophanês,
easily recognizable by reason of its famous crest. Or the
gray Calcar, certainly, or the equally interesting Eale,
with its tawny hide and rather remarkable antlers, which
were not only hollow as reeds, but movable. They
switched, just now, to catch the wind, which made a
mournful moaning song as it blew through them.

Mandricardo stared at the five monsters, and five
enormous, goggle-eyed heads rolled about to behold
him with a hungry gleam in each eye. You did not have
to be terribly clever in order to perceive that the thought
which moved through each and every head was the
same: Here comes Lunch.

The trick was, thought Mandricardo to himself, how
to get to the well, since you had to walk past the
grinning jaws of five extraordinary and hungry-looking
monstrosities to get there.

Well, he took the Carpet, of course. There is hardly
any point in having a Magic Flying Carpet along with

you on your quests and adventures if you are not going to use it. Carpets have feelings, after all. . . .

The five beasts, thus cruelly disappointed of their two-legged Snack, hooted, bellowed, hissed, or grumbled—each according to the manner of its kind—but the Tartar paid them no particular attention. He was fond of animals on the whole, was Mandricardo, but there *are* limits. And hardly anything likes to be anything else's Lunch.

The Carpet floated down to the hilltop, and he hopped off and approached the well. A low stone wall ran around it and two posts supported a little thatched roof over the mouth of the well as if to keep rainwater from getting mixed with the wellwater. Mandricardo fetched up the bucket, and using the dipper chained to the side of the well (the dipper was solid gold), took a cautious sip of the stuff.

It was cold and utterly delicious, with a *bouquet* that he had never discovered in any other water in all the world.

It never occurred to Mandricardo to wonder what sort of water might be so precious as to be in a well guarded by fabulous monsters.

Nor did he notice the letters cut in the stone about the lips of the well. These read:

FONS.

IUVENTUTUM.

Mandricardo swallowed the water from the well—and winked out of existence like a soap bubble which somebody had pricked.

His garments and armor and the lion-skins he wore slung about his shoulders fell in a disordered heap on the ground.

In this tangle of clothing there sat a very fat and quite naked baby.

Its chubby cheeks turned quite red and for a time it squalled lustily, balling fat little hands into tiny futile fists.

Moments later, having forgotten all about whatever had put it in such a rage, the baby blinked solemnly about it. Its gaze fell upon its fat pink toes. These it wriggled. Then it fell slowly over backward and began to try to put this fat pink toe and then that fat pink toe in its mouth.

Of Sir Mandricardo there was not the slightest sign.

20

The Famous Fountain

Only a very little time after Mandricardo and Callipygia and their beasts and baggage had flown out of the Roc's nest in that steep toboggan ride of theirs, Gorgonzola and Limburger arrived on a wish all the way from the mountains of the northerly parts of the Afric continent. And on their heels down flew the monstrous Marid, thirsty for blood and revenge.

They found the Roc's nest, of course, but it was empty, save for the Rocettes which goggled endearingly up at the huge winged genie as if wondering if he were or were not their mother. But there was nary Tartar nor Amazon to be found therein, neither was there a Magic Carpet anywheres about.

Gargling with fury, the Marid snatched a huge boulder from the peak of Mount Caucasus and crushed it to powder in his mighty fist.

"Where is the caitiff rogue and scoundrel?" he roared. And, let me tell you right now, when a Genie twenty times the size of a grown man roars at you, well, you

have been roared at. The roar knocked Gorgonzola flat on his back.

Picking himself up and scraping off a modicum of Roc guano, the Wicked Enchanter strove to placate the furious Genie by suggesting that perhaps, after all, the Roc's hatchlings had devoured the Tartar. To say nothing of his Amazon sweetheart, beasts, baggage, and Carpet to boot, since none of these were visible.

Before the Marid could make up his mind about that, a shadow fell over the mountain peak and a tremendous screech nearly blew Gorgonzola flat again. They looked up to see the mother Roc hurtling straight for them, immense claws outstretched to crunch and maim. She was screeching like the steam-whistle of a locomotive, for nothing infuriates a mother Roc more than somebody meddling about in her nest, especially when she has a brood of new hatchlings.

As for the Marid, he yelled in surprise and shot straight up in the air, clapping his huge black vulture-wings together like volleys of thunder. Even a powerful Marid thinks twice before picking a quarrel with an enraged mother Roc. Or a *father* Roc, for that matter.

The Roc broke her fall and swerved to meet the Marid, mistakenly thinking him to be the molester of her hatchlings. In the next instant, the air above Mount Caucasus was dark as the center of a stormcloud and the scene of as furious a battle between gigantic monsters as you might ever wish to see.

Gorgonzola did not in the least wish to see it. He would, I suppose, have come to the aid of the Marid with his enchantments, but at the moment he had his hands full. That is to say, when the Roc came down toward them like an avalanche of red-eyed fury, poor Limburger rolled his eyes up in his head, his complexion turned the color of library paste (it was already just about as lumpy), and he fainted dead away. If Gorgonzola had not caught him, his senseless servant might have fallen out of the Roc's nest and suffered considerable damage.

Moments later, the Marid, having had quite enough of battling against a maddened Roc, vanished from sight, melting away into thin air by means of a special skill known to Marids and Efreets. This would ordinarily have left it up to Gorgonzola to face the angry mother Roc alone, but he took a hasty swig from his copper bottle full of wishing potion and he and Limburger vanished, as well, leaving the mother Roc alone on the mountain-peak with her hungry, but otherwise unharmed, brood of Rocettes.

Now when Callipygia returned from her hunting, with several plump game-birds flung over her shoulder, and found Mandricardo gone and the Carpet, too, it did not take the Amazon girl very long to figure out where he and it had gotten to. That is to say, from where she happened to be standing she could clearly see the Magic Flying Carpet spread out, for some unearthly reason, atop the small hill that stood nearby, the one that had a stone well on it.

Toward this hill she trudged, and when she arrived at its foot and saw the five monsters chained to their posts, each of them eyeing her almost as if, in their goggling eyes, Callipygia was but a Morsel, she prudently decided that rather than disturbing such as the black-furred Bleps and the greater-crested Strycophanês, she would simply call up to Mandricardo, who must, after all, be somewhere atop the hill since the Carpet was there.

And so she called; but he neglected to reply, and instead there came from thereabouts the petulant crying of a small baby, which was absurd and which Callipygia put down, rather sensibly, to the distant crying of marsh-fowl which often sound uncannily like human infants. Well, she had told him to find water and he had located the nearest well, apparently; but, where had the great simpleton gotten himself to, that he could not hear her when she called his name?

And when was somebody going to stop that baby from crying?

There was nothing else to do, it seemed, but climb the hill and retrieve the Carpet—Callipygia could hardly leave it behind. And, while she was on the hilltop, she could look around for some clue as to wherever Mandricardo had gotten himself to. Perhaps the huge booby had simply fallen down the well. . . .

She approached the first beast, which was the celebrated Bleps, and stood for a moment, admiring its sleek and handsome black fur and measuring the width of its froglike mouth and the hunger in those yellow and burning and goggling eyes. Then she took one of the game-birds she had brought down with her bow and tossed it to the monster, for all the world as a housewife tosses a bone to the dog. The Bleps caught it in midair and began to crunch it between his heavy tushes; while the creature was thus occupied, Callipygia scuttled past his station, safe and unscathed.

The next beast in order was the remarkable Strycophanês, and it responded with the same alacrity as had the fearsome Bleps when she tossed the second of her game-birds to him. In no time, the Strycophanês was engaged in grinding the bird's bones to powder, never noticing that Callipygia had passed its station also unscathed.

With the third of the fabulous beasts, it was the same, and the Amazon reflected to herself that, rare and unique and legended though these creatures undoubtedly were, they did not happen to be very bright. She also thanked Providence that, since there hap-

pened to be five of the monsters, she had coinciden-
tally brought down five birds.

Reaching the safety of the well, she paused to catch
her breath and to look around. The heaped and scattered garments that belonged to Mandricardo, and the
pieces of his armor, boots and weapons, baffled her
only momentarily. For no sooner had she seen the fat,
naked baby, bawling hungrily amidst the clothing and
saw the inscription around the lip of the well, then she
knew the worst.

Apparently the daughters of the Queen of the country of the Amazons are tutored in a broader curriculum
than are the children of the King of Tartary; for, where
Mandricardo had only been instructed in Greek, among
the ancient languages, Callipygia had received sufficient tutoring in Latin to know what

FONS.
IUVENTUTEM.

or Fons Juventutem, as in Latin "iu" is interchangeable
with "j", means.

"Oh, my," she sighed, and, rather helplessly picked
up the squalling infant. Seating herself on the edge of
the Fountain of Youth, she dangled the baby on her
knee and could not help noticing what a fat and healthy
child her Tartar lover had been when he was about
seven weeks old.

She was still occupied with these thoughts, a few
moments later, when Gorgonzola snapped into existence on the hilltop and regarded her with menace in
his cold black eyes.

The Old Man Who Looks After Cockaigne was in the
backyard of his hut hoeing his cabbages, when the
Tarandus came strolling up the lane to pay him a visit.

Where you or I would have stopped and stared to see a Tarandus—or, as I should more properly say, *the* Tarandus, for there is only one of them, yes, even here in Cockaigne—the Old Man merely glanced up from his hoeing, said, "You again, is it?" and returned to his labors.

The Tarandus took this inhospitable greeting in its stride, curled up on the grass beside the cabbage patch and proceeded to groom its whiskers. As it left the road, the dun-colored creature became entirely green, yes, even to the whites of its eyes. This was because the Tarandus, whom the better-thought-of Bestiaries *will* persist in calling "opal-colored" even when he is nothing of the sort, had been designed by whatever playful caprice of Nature had done the job, more or less along the lines of the common chameleon. Which is to say that the neutral-hued creature always assumed the coloration of whatever background he stood in front of, if you take my meaning.

"They are bothering the beasts, over there at the Fountain," said the Tarandus to the Old Man Who Looks After Cockaigne.

"They are, are they?" replied the Old Man Who Looks After Cockaigne to the Tarandus. "And who might *they* be, pray tell?"

"A Tartar knight, an Amazon girl, and a Wicked Enchanter," said the Tarandus, lazily beginning to clean its left ear. It is a highly intelligent beast, the Tarandus, quite unlike its five fellows who spent their days chained up to guard the approach to the famous Fountain, and who were, as Callipygia had already discovered for herself, rather obtuse and dull-witted. I call the Tarandus pretty shrewd to have realized at a guess that the Wicked Enchanter was a Wicked Enchanter; Mr. Sherlock Holmes could not have done it better.

At this news the Old Man straightened up and tugged

at his beard, which was stiff and bristly. He looked unhappy.

"Well, I suppose I have to go and see about it, then," he said grumpily. "If They had consulted *me*, I could have told Them not to put the Fountain so kind of out in the open like that, where just about any riffraff could come along and discover it. Have the beasts eaten them, do you know? The strangers, I mean?"

Curled on the green grass, the green Tarandus yawned, revealing a green tongue, of course, and replied: "No, they have not. The first arrival flew over their heads on some sort of rug; the second fed a fat bird to each of my greedy brethren and skipped past him while he was occupied with dining off the gift. The third one appeared out of thin air, as the saying goes."

"Hmmph," commented the Old Man Who Looks After Cockaigne. "And you just happened to be passing by when all this happened, I suppose."

"Not exactly. I was bored and thought that I would go and visit my fellow beasts. They are as much one-of-a-kind as I am, you know, and that means we are very lonely. While they are chained together and have, therefore, company all around to talk to, I, as you no doubt are aware, live alone and prefer it that way. But it *does* get lonely. . . ."

"I will chain you up beside your friends if you like," offered the Old Man, but the Tarandus shook its head very positively.

"No, I think not. I am of solitary habits and retiring disposition, and the chatter of so many empty-headed creatures would get on my nerves terribly. They are all right to talk to once in a while, but to be in their company all the time would fret me to distraction."

"Well, I'd better be getting over there before they've drunk the Fountain dry," said the Old Man, and he rested the handle of his hoe against the back wall of his cottage, took up a shapeless hat and a comfortable old coat, put these on, and headed around the house for the lane. "Are you coming?" he asked.

The Tarandus shook its his head. "I think I will go over and visit the Syl and the Soham instead," answered the creature, and without further ado, faded away.

"Suit yourself," shrugged the Old Man Who Looks After Cockaigne. "Pesky creature!" he added.

BOOK FIVE

Ithuriel

21

Disenchanting Mandricardo

"Who," inquired Callipygia, "are you?" My reader will remember that neither she nor Mandricardo had at this time encountered the Wicked Enchanter face to face, although the Tartar knight had glimpsed him once across the room in the carpet-monger's storeroom. And Mandricardo was presently in no condition to point him out to Callipygia.

"That is neither here nor there, my wench," spat the other, advancing upon the Amazon girl with pantherine tread, one clawed hand outstretched as if to scratch her eyes out. She could not help noticing that his wicked black eyes seemed to be spitting red sparks.

"All right, then," said Callipygia belligerently. "Try *this* question on for size, then—what the devil do you want?"

She was in no mood, just then, for being bothered by meddlesome strangers, was our Callipygia. Here was her lover suddenly transformed into a fat baby—and a very hungry one, at that—and, to make matters worse, she had just discovered that he needed changing (not that he was wearing anything to change). Callipygia was no stranger to babies, not with sixteen sisters and more than a few of them married and mothers themselves, but she was going through a difficult and trying time, just now, and this nosy tall man with the glaring black eyes would just *have* to come sticking his nose in where he wasn't wanted . . . and her with her hands full of squalling baby, and, wouldn't you just know? not a bottle or a clean diaper for half a kingdom round, most likely.

Gorgonzola, seizing his opportunity, advanced upon her with lithe and pard-like tread, his eyes spitting red sparks. This was his moment, and he intended to seize it by the forelock, as you might say. The mysterious Mandricardo, with his unknown magical powers, or, at least, Gorgonzola thought he had magical powers, was for some reason nowhere to be seen: there was only this fat, frumpy female and her yelling brat between him and the Magic Flying Carpet.

"That Carpet," he hissed, advancing on her. He was close enough by now so that she could see that his eyes really *were* spitting red-hot sparks; even as she watched, one fell on the collar of his robe and singed a hole right through it. "Step aside, wench—I want that Carpet!"

"Oh, *this* Carpet?" asked Callipygia, pretending innocence. Then she put the baby down on the Carpet behind her and stood on it herself, legs spread, folding her arms and interposing her not-inconsiderable self between the Wicked Enchanter and the thing he craved. As she stood there with folded arms, one hand was playing fretfully with the curious old bronze ring she wore about her upper arm, you remember, the one she had found in the Troll's cupboard.

"That Carpet is my property, and I mean to have it back," he said, and he ground his teeth together—an unnerving sound that rather put Callipygia's own teeth on edge. "Some lout of a Tartar stole it from me, the thieving rascal—"

"Oh, you must be this Gorgonzola who has been causing such a lot of bother down in Upper and Lower Pamphyllia," she said. "I'd been wondering when you were going to turn up again. Well, you aren't getting *this* Carpet, so be off with you!"

"Madame, if I have to drag you off the Carpet by your hair, and kick that ugly brat of yours out of the way, I'll not scruple," began the Wicked Enchanter nastily, but Callipygia, just then, had completely run out of patience. "Ugly brat," forsooth—and just when she had been thinking what a lovely fat baby her lover had once been!

Irritably twisting the bronze ring about and about on her upper arm, she snorted: "Oh, bother you and your wishes! *I* wish you were on the other side of the Moon!"

Whereupon, in point of fact—and very swiftly—*he was*. That mysterious bronze ring of Callipygia's simply didn't fool around: a wish is a wish seems to sum up the gist of the matter.

Poor Gorgonzola! For, you know, come to think of it, and taking all in all, he was not without a few sterling qualities—for a fiend, that is. He was tenacious; he was resourceful; and not without a certain bravery. Ah, well . . . . one wonders what his next thought was, finding himself where Callipygia had wished him to be. *Surprised*, simply isn't the proper word, I would hazard the guess.

And whatever other emotions must have gone seething through his breast, disgruntlement and chagrin must surely have been among them: for so swiftly and suddenly was he transported thither, that the abruptness of his transition somehow jarred loose that copper bottle of his, the one with the wishing-potion in it.

The bottle rolled out of sight in some of the taller weeds that grew beside the stone wall which encircled the famous Fountain, and nobody at all paid any attention to it, then or for very long after.

So much for Gorgonzola; it is just as well, I suppose, that he is now out of our story entirely, and we need no longer worry for fear that he will somehow wreak *a horrible revenge* on Doucelette and Florizel. . . .

Whether or not Gorgonzola was astonished, Callipygia certainly was. Her jaw dropped and she paled beneath her healthy tan, looking quickly around. But he was gone, no doubt about it.

As for Limburger, well, he gasped, turned up his eyes, and fainted dead away. This made the second time in this story that Limburger fainted, and I'm sorry to say that I think he was a little too nervous to be going around with Wicked Enchanters and evil genies and that sort. *That* is what you might call "life in the fast lane," and it requires a stronger and more durable constitution than Limburger's to keep up the pace.

However, as Limburger passes out of our story very shortly, it's a moot point. One hopes, thereafter, having learned his lesson, he avoids the company of enchanters and finds a secure niche in some lucrative, honest trade. Well, we can always hope.

It was not very long after this that Callipygia found the means to break Mandricardo's enchantment, or to nullify his transformation, or whatever the correct term is for one who has been accidentally youthened (if there is such a word, and if there isn't, there should be, for just such occasions as this); youthened, as I was saying, by having accidentally drunk of the waters of Fons Juventutem. He recovered his former appearance and age and everything, and at the moment the transformation occurred, had obviously been in the middle of swearing by devils again, for he regained his normal self in the midst of saying, "I say, by Apsu's ankles and by the stomach of Set and by the vocal cords of Vukub-Kakix, what—!"

Then, rather suddenly, realizing that he was himself again, and also that he was lying there stark naked, he crimsoned, snatched up his lion-skins and draped them about his middle parts, saying plaintively, and rather incoherently, "Oh, now, I say, dash it all, Cally, I mean, what? Give a felly a word of warning, can't you, what, old girl, eh?"

She politely turned her back while he climbed into his garments again as hurriedly as possible, and if you have never happened to see a knight half-in and half-out of his armor, hopping about on one leg while trying to get the other into a sheet-metal nether garment, well, it is quite a sight to behold.

When he was all together again and decent, they embraced and kissed rather enthusiastically and began babbling questions to each other and so on, at such a rate that neither of them could understand what it was that the other one was trying to say.

It was while this was going on that Limburger, having recovered from his swoon, decided to slip away. He left the scene by the remarkably simple method of running away—and the beasts of fable watched him run past them, and they blinked puzzledly, and did nothing at all to stop him, or even try to seize him, for, after all, they had been chained up in this place for the single purpose of keeping people from going *up* the hill to where the famous Fountain was. But nobody had ever told them to interfere with people who happened to be going *down* the hill, and that is why they did not bother Limburger.

He nearly fainted again from relief, took to his heels,

and very rapidly passed out of this scene and, in fact, out of our story entirely.

Not a bad fellow, Limburger, taking it all in all. Deplorable taste in employers, of course, but then, one cannot always pick and choose, can one?

While Limburger was engaged in dwindling into the distance, Mandricardo and Callipygia were busy hugging and kissing and all that sort of thing that parted lovers tend to do, rather enthusiastically, when their sundered paths are joined once again. They were also talking rapidly to each other between these hugs and kisses. The Amazon girl was telling him all about how she had returned from scaring up some lunch only to find him gone, and how she had followed him here and found him gone, and then how that really irritating Wicked Enchanter had come along, and so on, while Mandricardo was saying that he had only come over here to fetch some bally water, what, and how in the world (now that he came to think of it) did she get by the beasts, what, since she didn't have the Magic Flying Carpet, what, and she told him how she had employed what was originally intended to be their lunch (that is, the five fat game-birds) to the purpose of distracting the monsters; and he remarked that that was dashed clever of her, and so on.

When she got around to mentioning the Wicked Enchanter and how he had menaced her before vanishing so welcomely, but also so inexplicably, Mandricardo was interested.

"Oh, I say, not that rotter caused all the fuss down in Upper Pamphyllia, not to mention Lower Pamphyllia . . . bally old Gorgonwhatzizname?"

She informed him that such was the case. "The very one," nodded the Amazon girl. "Wanted your nice Car-

pet, he did, and was going to turn me into a toad, I
suppose, unless I gave it to him—"

Sir Mandricardo was quite put out to learn this.

"The cad," he said, ruffled that even a Wicked
Enchanter—and everyone knows what *they* are like—
would go sneaking up on girls, what, tryin' to snatch
one's Magic Carpet away from one. Such things *simply
weren't done*, not done at all, at least in the best
circles, anyway.

Mandricardo paid no attention to the fact that it was,
after all, from this same Wicked Enchanter that he had
purloined the article in question in the first place, back
in Chapter Five. Had you happened to have brought
this interesting, but ultimately irrelevent, fact to his
attention, I have little doubt but what he would have
brushed it aside like an annoying fly, remarking something to the effect of, hem, a mere detail, that, I mean,
the *principle* of the thing—!

"Wish I'd been there, old girl, what," he declared
stoutly. "I'd have taught the rotter not to go slinkin'
around threatenin' delicately-nurtured women and tryin'
to pinch a felly's Carpet, deuced if I wouldn't."

"Well, you *were* there, of course, it's only that you
weren't—*you* . . . in a manner of speaking," Callipygia,
rather confusedly (and, also, rather confusingly, for it
was obvious that Mandricardo didn't have the faintest
idea of what she was talking about). For it suddenly
occurred to the Amazon girl that, quite possibly, even
quite likely, her betrothed did not at all remember
having been transformed into a fat baby by the famous
Fountain. So she explained to him all about the thing,
and its properties, and the inscription in Latin, and all.

Well, he was quite dumbfounded. At least, he certainly *looked* dumbfounded.

"Do you mean to say that I—I mean, dash it!—that it
was the dratted *Fountain of*—? Well, I'll be dashed! I'd

no idea, you know, what—thought the bally thing was just an old *well*—well, of course, *Latin*—I mean, dash it all, bally Latin and all, *hic*, *haec*, *hoc*, and all that sort of rot—!"

I have little doubt that Sir Mandricardo would have been fully capable of burbling on in this manner for at least a half a page more, had not Callipygia flung her arms about him at this point. Whereupon, rather naturally, there ensued yet another round of the hugging-and-kissing, until time was called for both to recover their breath.

And it was very shortly after this that the Old Man Who Looks After Cockaigne arrived on the scene and they would have had to stop all the hugging-and-kissing anyway, in order to pay attention to this new visitor, had they not already completed the latest bout . . . and I will take the opportunity afforded by his arrival to close the chapter at this point, if you have no objections, and save the scene of his introduction to our hero and heroine until the next episode.

22

A Luncheon in Cockaigne

Now he came huffing and puffing up the road, muttering to himself as very old people sometimes do and complaining about the steepness of the way, although the fact of the matter was that he suffered from a certain shortness of breath. And had it not been for the faded and patched and rather dilapidated old clothes that he wore, you would have thought him a personage of considerable importance, from the way that the Bleps and the Strycophanês fawned upon him and licked his heels, yes, and the gray Calcar, too, as well as the Eale with the movable horns, and that is not to mention the Leucrocotta with her golden mane and nicely-matching whiskers.

Mandricardo was impressed. "I say, Cally, look! Bally beasts don't seem to be tryin' to gobble him up, what?"

"Well, of course they aren't," grumbled the Old Man as he came up to where they were standing on the top of the little hill right next to the famous Fountain, for old or no, the Old Man rejoiced in excellent hearing and had caught Mandricardo's remark to Callipygia. "Of course they aren't," he was saying, "for who do you think feeds the poor beasts, anyway? Somebody would have to, wouldn't they now, or else the miserable creatures would starve to death, chained to those posts the way they are. And they would be stupid indeed if they didn't recognize their keeper, now wouldn't they? Of course, today I'll probably skimp on their meal since the lady here has already fed them on fat birds, as the Tarandus mentioned."

They looked at him curiously, but no more curiously than he was examining them.

"Don't very often get Amazons or Tartars here in Cockaigne, we don't," he said after a bit.

Callipygia started and began to look around interestedly.

"Oh, are we in Cockaigne?" she inquired delightedly. "Well, I had no idea—no idea at all. True, I did notice that the sunlight seemed richer, somehow, more golden and all; and the trees looked older, more quaintly gnarled than usual, and those hills over there—Cockaigne! Fancy that, Mandri!"

"Right-ho," he nodded agreeably. "Cockaigne, what? Capital, capital! Never been there, meself."

But the Old Man Who Looks After Cockaigne wasted no more time with this sort of persiflage, if persiflage is quite the word I want: he got straight to business.

"Now, we simply cannot have people messing around with our famous Fountain," he said severely. "We are very proud of our Fountain here in Cockaigne, you know, and . . . but I could have sworn that the Tarandus said there were three of you. Wasn't there a Wicked Enchanter, too? I could have sworn that the Tarandus said something about there being a Wicked Enchanter."

Callipygia put his mind to rest on this point.

"Yes, there certainly was," she said, nodding. "By

the name of Gorgonzola; wanted back in Upper and
Lower Pamphyllia on at least two counts of wicked
enchantment, conjuring up dangerous elementals and
that sort of thing. But he vanished just a little while
before I disenchanted Mandricardo."

"Vanished, you say? How odd!" mused the Old Man
Who Looks After Cockaigne. "They don't usually vanish, you know. We've had more than our share of
trouble from Wicked Enchanters . . . what with the
Fountain, and all, you understand."

"Well, *this* one just up and vanished," she assured
him. "Quite frankly, I've no idea why; I was rather busy
with Mandricardo at the time, needing his diapers
changed and so on—not that he was wearing any at the
time, of course, but just the same—"

At this point, the Tartar knight cleared his throat
loudly and said, "Yes, well! Hem! Sure the Old Man
Who Looks After Such-and-Such isn't interested in such
matters, m'love . . . and I was just wonderin' however
did you change me back to my former self, if you know
what I mean—?"

"As a matter of fact, I have been wondering about
that, myself," admitted the Old Man, looking interestedly at the Amazon girl, who flushed prettily.

"Well, there was really nothing to it, nothing at all.
Simplicity itself, you might well say," said Callipygia
modestly. "When I was studying my lessons as a girl,
my tutors gave me a course in Elementary Thauma-
turgy, and I just happened to remember that to repeat
a spell the second time will usually erase the effects of
saying it the first time. And I wondered if this was true
of enchantments, like the one poor Mandricardo was
under—except that he made the *sweetest* baby! You
should have seen his chubby little legs!"

"Ahem, yes-yes! Sure the gentleman isn't interested
in *that* sort of thing, m'love," said Mandricardo, inter-

rupting hastily, the tips of his ears going bright red. "Do get on with it, old girl!"

"Well, there really isn't very much more to tell. I just poured another dipperful of water from that famous Fountain of yours into the baby's mouth, and—and it worked."

"And deuced clever of you it was, old girl," said Mandricardo fondly. Even the Old Man had to agree with this.

"Yes, quite ingenious, I must say, Madame Callipygia. If I hadn't already known how to reverse the powers of the Fountain (which I already knew, of course, since, after all, I am in charge of it, you know, just as I am in charge of everything else here in Cockaigne), I really don't think I would have thought of it. A second dose cancels out the effects of the first . . . very clever notion. And tell me, by the way, and while we are on the subject of your most recent adventures and perils, do you happen to have seen a gigantic green-skinned Genie anywheres about?"

The two, rather puzzledly, confessed that, happily, they had not; why? So the Old Man Who Looks After Cockaigne told them all about how Gorgonzola had villainously sought to inveigle a notoriously short-tempered Marid into going after them, by lying to the monster. He also explained how the Marid had appeared in mid-air above the peak of Mount Caucausus only moments after they had flown away therefrom aboard the Magic Flying Carpet and how he had gotten into an aerial battle with the mother Roc, who had driven him off, at least temporarily.

They swore feelingly on this topic and gave voice to one or two disparaging remarks on the personal cleanliness, parentage and private habits of Gorgonzola which would probably have made that gentleman blush, had he been present to have heard them.

"Well, it's no great fun to have angry Marids after one, I should think!" said the Old Man Who Looks After Cockaigne. "He was one Akhdar the Green, by the way, a very powerful and most dangerous Marid, whom the enchanter Gorgonzola taunted into getting angry at you on the pretext that you had said several very unpleasant things about him. This was, I suppose, Gorgonzola's notion of revenge . . . paying you back for rescuing Princess Doucelette from his unsavory attentions."

Callipygia glanced at the Old Man curiously, wondering, much as did Mandricardo, how he knew so much of what had recently been happening to them. Then it occurred to her that he might very well be one of the Léshy, which would explain a lot of things. And, after all, he must be a personage with rather important connections in the Right Place, in order to be deemed worthy to Look After Cockaigne, and who better than one of the Léshy? So she left unvoiced the question that trembled upon her lips.

And this was probably wise of her. After all, like many other personages of importance, the Léshy enjoy their little incognitos.

"Dare say we'll have a bit of trouble with that rotter, what, once he gets over being pecked half to pieces by the Roc," ventured Mandricardo cautiously.

"Not necessarily," said the Old Man reassuringly. "Marids, like other immortals, have very short memories; they have to, you see, for with lives so long they would otherwise accumulate a crushing burden of things to remember. Why, they can't even carry a grudge for long.*"

---

* Akhdar must have been the exception that proved the rule, then, for he was still at this time harboring a grudge against Gorgonzola, who had, you will remember, either stolen from him or somehow cheated him out of certain smaragdines. The Chronicle Narrative doesn't say which.

"Good-oh; but let's hope you're right, what," muttered the Tartar knight. He sounded unconvinced, and after all, if someone has gotten a gigantic and vicious-tempered Genie mad at one, one has a right to worry just a mite.

It was, by then somewhat past mid-day, and Mandricardo's stomach was at the moment reminding him that it had seen no sign of lunch. He mentioned this to his companions.

"Well, let's take the Carpet and leave this hill to its monsters," suggested Callipygia practically, "and I'll see what I can do about bringing down a few more fat game-birds for lunch—"

"Nonsense, my dear," said the Old Man firmly. "The two of you will come home with me and be my guests for lunch. Come, I won't hear another word! Rough, simple fare, but it will be satisfying, I assure you, and there is no food better than simple fare."

So it was decided, and they went back to the Old Man's cottage for their lunch.

The travelers found the Old Man's cottage quite snug and comfy, with plenty of hot water for washing up and nice soft towels. A huge iron kettle of succulent cabbage soup was simmering on the hearth, and besides bowls of this, they had ham and boiled potatoes and mugs of strong tea, and found the meal, as advertised, simple but hearty.

As for the furnishings of the cottage, well, perhaps the less said of them the better. Mandricardo did not at all like the stuffed Corkodrill which hung stiffly from chains suspended from the beams of the roof; that is, he did not like the way the thing's bright red glass eyes followed them about the one room of the cottage, and at one point the long jaws of the stuffed Corkodrill opened a bit and Mandricardo had the rather horrible notion that the creature was almost on the point of entering into their conversation, which was about nothing very important, but was not to be interrupted by mere stuffed Corkodrills.

And, when they compared notes later, he learned that Callipygia felt similarly uneasy about the fire on the hearth, which burned with flames of blue and green and purple, unlike more wholesome and ordinary fires, and also unlike these, it burned *without any visible fuel*.

On the other hand, the Old Man was an excellent host, and his conversation matched the bill of fare, in that it was honest and simple and satisfying, without being in the least fancy or high-faluting, whatever that means; it does not happen to be in my dictionary, I don't know about yours. They conversed mostly about Cockaigne and its rare and curious fauna. Of course they would be discussing the fauna, since the flora of Cockaigne has nothing about it that is especially noteworthy.

"Yes, quite a few interesting and unusual animals have taken up Cockaigne for their residence," the Old Man was saying, puffing away on his Meerschaum pipe (which was in itself unusual, since tobacco had not yet been invented, much less Meerschaum pipes!). You have already, of course, met my friends the Bleps and the Strycophanês, the Calcar, to say nothing of the Eale and the Leucrocotta; and besides these we have currently on hand here in Cockaigne the remarkable Tarandus, as well as the Syl and the Soham, the Catoblepas and an entire flock (or perhaps I should say, pack) of Senmurvs—"

"Very interesting, what," mumbled Mandricardo, stifling a yawn with a polite palm. "Good huntin' hereabout, what?"

"Goodness gracious, we don't permit hunting here," said the Old Man crossly.

"Oh, I say! Not at all?"

"Certainly not. So very many of our more notable fauna are not only rare but completely unique, that hunting would be the very least sport we should encourage here in Cockaigne. . . ."

"Talk about your endangered species, eh?" remarked Callipygia, smothering a yawn of her own. "Mandri? I do think we should be getting on our way, now that we are finished with the delicious lunch this kind gentleman was so generous to share with us. . . ."

"Quite right m'dear, what-ho for the open road, what?" said the Tartar knight, cheerfully.

"Well, if you're quite sure you've had enough," said the Old Man anxiously. "I often feel that young people do not pay proper attention to their diet, you know . . . with them, it's all gobble-it-down-and-run. And there remains plenty more cabbage soup in the pot, not to mention the boiled ham—?"

23

Ithuriel Interrupts

They said their goodbyes to the Old Man, who pressed upon them a package containing some raw potatoes they could bake over coals, a hefty slab of boiled ham, and a jar of cold cabbage soup.

"Just tuck this in your picnic hamper," he said gruffly, "and let's have no more talk about it! Like to see young people *eat*, I do; always have!"

"Very kind of your honor, I'm sure," said Mandricardo. "Now, if you'll just direct us to Amazonia, what, we'll be gettin' along."

"Yes, in which part of the world *is* Cockaigne, presently?" asked Callipygia. She and Mandricardo, being natives to Terra Magica, were of course familiar with the fact that it was somewhat different from most other countries, insofar as while they remain comfortably in one place age after age, it restlessly peregrinates, for some reason known only to They who created it in the first place.

"Ah, well, now, in that respect, my dear Princess,

you could hardly be more fortunate," he assured her comfortably. For as it turns out—and I am often favorably impressed at how neatly these things turn out, sometimes, that is, anyway—at the very moment Cockaigne is adjacent to the country of the Amazons; yes," he added, pointing off into the roseate distance, "that metallic glinting over there is the famous river Thermodon, which, as I do not have to tell *you*, my dear, flows directly through the country of the Amazons, and upon whose very shores is the capital, Themiscyra."

"Gadzooks!" exclaimed Mandricardo, starting a little and preening his moustaches zestfully. "Bit of good luck, what, Cally, m'girl?"

She agreed that the most recent peregrination of Cockaigne, from the eastern foothills surrounding Mount Caucasus to this particular region of Pontus, near the shores of the Euxine Sea, which was the vicinity of Amazonia, was fortuitous in the extreme. They had, in effect, traveled four hundred leagues due east—the direction in which they wanted to travel, anyway.

"Yes, yes; but I would advise you to waste no time in crossing our borders and hastening to swim or ford the Thermodon," said the Old Man Who Looks After Cockaigne, "for we are likely to depart from this region at any moment, and if you delay your departure unduly, you may well find yourselves on the shores of the Frozen Sea, or in the parched deserts of Afric being glibbered to by the uncouth and timid Troglodytes—"

He accompanied them as far as the crossroads, chattily giving them additional directions and advice and such like every step of the way. A garrulous old gentleman, the Old Man Who Looks After Cockaigne, but hospitable to a fault.

*   *   *

Both of their horses, to say nothing of the plump little mule, had enjoyed a good long respite from the road, due to these recent adventures, so they were fresh and spirited as colts. It was not very long before they reached the borders where Cockaigne ended and Pontus began and crossed over, finding themselves on the shores of the Thermodon, whose broad silvery floods glided by in stately and dignified fashion, under a late afternoon sky.

As it was too broad to swim and too deep to ford, they cantered along beside it for some little time, hoping to find a ferryman, if not a bridge, but encountering neither. Then it was that Mandricardo smote his brow with the palm of one hand, in disgust at the shortness of his own memory.

"Oh, I say, Cally . . . stupid of me. I forgot all about the bally old Carpet, dash it!" he exclaimed.

"Don't blame yourself, my hero," she grinned rather sheepishly, "for I forgot it, too. Well, unpack it and let's get over into Amazonia . . . as I recall this stretch of the river, we've a dozen leagues to go before we reach the nearest ferry."

Mandricardo sprang from the saddle and unstrapped the Carpet, which had been neatly rolled up and stored away along with their other gear on Minerva's back. He was just spreading the Magic Flying Carpet on the ground and smoothing out the wrinkles in preparation for all of them climbing aboard, when there was a deafening clap of thunder, the sky darkened, a whirlwind blew sand in their eyes and Mandricardo's cloak over his head, and a gigantic form, dark as a stormcloud, sprang up before them. Three red eyes glared in its scowling visage, like meteors in a thundercloud, and it gnashed its tusks like an unfuriated oliphant.

"Despicable varlet! Prepare to meet your doom,"

roared a voice that could have split boulders. Both horses bolted, pelting away in two different directions, and, as for the little mule, she rolled up her eyes and fainted on the spot.

"Oh, Mandri!" wailed Callipygia. "It's—it's—!"

"It is I, Akhdar the Green! Now you shall regret having abused my good name with your lies and boastings," thundered the mighty Marid, and, bending over, he stretched forth a hand big enough to play dice with farmhouses in the direction of the Tartar knight, who, his face still muffled in the folds of his windblown cloak, struggled to free himself and to draw his trusty steel.

"*Wait!*" screeched Callipygia, springing forward and intrepidly interposing her person between the monstrous green hand and the Tartar knight, who, sword drawn but head still wrapped in that dashed cloak, was turned completely about, swinging sharp steel at empty air and shouting, "Have at you, sir! Take that, you caitiff rogue, what!" in muffled tones.

The green hand hovered.

Three eyes like balls of red fire glared down through the whirlwind.

"Well?" demanded the Marid in a voice like thunder.

"It was not Mandricardo who defamed your name and swore to battle you," she yelled up to the Marid, who bent closer in order to hear her tiny voice over the wind's roaring.

"Then who did?" inquired the Marid, skeptically.

"That villainous Gorgonzola," Callipygia declared. "He wished Mandricardo destroyed, but feared to do the deed himself, timorous of his safety when faced with so valorous a knightly champion. So he tricked you, deceiving you with sly and cunning words, tempting you into a fury of rage against one who had not until just recently even had knowledge of your very existence. O mighty Marid," she added by way of polite afterthought.

"Hmm," said the Marid, scowling. It contorted its brow in an effort of thought; either the process was painful, or the brow was not accustomed to being contorted. Perhaps both.

For a moment he chewed the idea over—then he spat it out. In point of fact, he opened his enormous jaws and expectorated a thirty-foot-long jet of fiery sulphur and brimstone, by way of a gentle indication of his mood.

"Bah!" snorted Akhdar disgustedly. "What do you take me for, anyway, madame? Some sort of a simpleton? This Gorgonzola, Wicked Enchanter or no Wicked Enchanter, would hardly go to all the effort to think up so elaborate a concoction of untruths when he could obliterate this human cockroach as easily as I do now—"

And he balled his birdclawed fingers into a fist heavy enough to pound medium-sized mountains into molehills with, and for a moment it hovered over Mandricardo's head, while Callipygia drew in and held her breath, thinking to herself what a pity that the Old Man Who Looks After Cockaigne had been so dreadfully wrong about Marids and their short memories.

Mandricardo, his cloak by now caught on an attachment or link fastened to his armor, so that it would take both hands to free his face from the clinging folds of cloth, had tripped over his own helmet, which had itself fallen off a moment before, and he had fallen prone, the sword flying from his fingers. He was completely unaware, of course, that several tons of Maridfist hovered above him, momentarily about to crush him into a greasespot.

"*What,*" inquired a deep, ponderous voice in gentle tones, "*is going on here?*" Although quietly phrased, the question had about it somehow the weight of Authority.

Both Callipygia and Marid looked up.

Standing up to his ankles in the gliding floods of the silvery Thermodon stood another stupendous figure—this one being somewhat more stupendous than that of the green-skinnned Marid, the Amazon girl quickly noted—and this one enormously less ugly and ferocious-looking.

Where Akhdar's shoulders sprouted with the black and stinking wings of a monstrous vulture, the wings that grew from the broad shoulders of the stranger (which shoulders, by the way, were clad in glittering steel armor picked out with several thousand quite excellent blue-white diamonds of the finest water)—from the shoulders of the stranger, as I was saying, grew wings whose feathers were the indigo and emerald and bronze plumes of a peacock's tail.

Instead of the black-browed and scowling visage of Akhdar, crowned with horrible antlers and glaring about with its burning three-eyed gaze, the stranger's features were of Classical, even superhuman beauty, not unlike those of an Archangel; golden curls crowned his noble brow, as white as alabaster, and his gaze fell from calm, pellucid eyes as blue as sapphires.

Instead of a horrid spiked iron mace, he held the hilt of a mighty sword whose blade was nothing less than a crackling bolt of lightning.

The Marid wilted, gaped, faltered. Three eyes like globes of sanguine fire rolled in terror. It was more than obvious to Callipygia that the newcomer held either superior rank or superior prowess to the Marid, or, quite likely, both.

"O Ithuriel, Great Prince of the Genii," said the Marid sullenly, "I but visit my rightful vengeance upon treacherous and boastful mortals who have made my name a synonym for cowardice and, also, somewhat of a laughing-stock in the Spirit World—"

"Where, prior to these events, it, of course, enjoyed

the highest esteem," commented the great Genie, with more than a touch of sarcasm in his even tones.

Akhdar the Green flushed under the sting in this mild rebuke, and Callipygia was interested to learn, when someone who is green-skinned blushes, his or her skin turns an even deeper shade of green. In Akhdar's case, the shade was a particularly pretty one of olive-green.

"Well, well, and be that as it may," said the Marid hastily, and slightly ill-temperedly, "but it does not alter the fact that I am within my rights in visting my vengeance upon the—"

"Don't be silly, you contentious Marid, you have neither right nor authority nor power in these parts of the world," said the great Genie in solemn tones . . . and we shall delay until the next (and last, at least in this history) chapter the full measure of his judgment.

24

Across the Thermodon

"Don't be silly, you contentious Marid," Prince Ithuriel was saying just then, "you have neither right nor authority nor any particular power at all in these parts of the world. For these, you must know, are not the Mountains of the Moon, but the realms adjacent to and coterminous with the famous Empire of the Persians, and, in other words, you find yourself in those regions of the world which Her Majesty Getiafrose, Queen of All the Genii, had placed under my jurisdiction and sway."

"But—" said Akhdar.

"There are no buts," said Ithuriel severely. "Therefore, begone from these parts, O Akhdar the Green, and visit your vaunted vengeance*—if visit it you really must—upon that despicable and prevaricatious enchanter, Gorgonzola, who has tricked you, deceived you, and

---

* Please note that one very seldom has the opportunity to use so many words beginning with "v" in an ordinary sentence.

played you for a fool . . . not that Nature has not already cast you in that precise role!"

With a howl of fury that split the welkin, whatever a welkin is, the Marid stamped one tremendous foot. The earth shuddered and broke asunder; a fountain of roaring fire thundered skyward; Akhdar turned and dove into the flaming cleft in the earth, which swallowed him as the Whale did Jonah: the earthen lips closed together again and left all more or less as it had been only a moment or two before.

Callipygia said nothing, but thought to herself that it was certainly dramatic, the way the Genii kept appearing and disappearing with such extraordinary effects.

"Great Prince Ithuriel," she said—for Mandricardo was still lurching around with his back to what was going on and his cloak over his head, swinging his broadsword lustily, but cleaving empty air—"Great Prince Ithuriel, how very fortunate we are that you just happened along in the very moment to prevent the murderous Marid from—"

But he was shaking his huge head, golden locks stirring beneath his great helm of polished steel.

"It was," said Ithuriel gravely, making her a gentle courtesy, "neither luck nor accident that I came by, and chance played no part in the matter. No, it was my good and respected friend, the Old Man Who Looks After Cockaigne, who happened to bring to my attention only a few minutes ago that one of the Marids of sultry Afric was loose in those dominions which are under my protection; I resolved to look into the matter without further delay. As for Akhdar the Green, I assure you, madame, that you need fear no more this temperish and overly gullible Marid, who will bother you and your betrothed no longer. And now, if you will forgive me, I must depart, for the nations under my demesne are many and quarrelsome, and even as we

speak, I perceive a border skirmish between the Medes
and the Scythians which demands my earliest attention—"

And with another deep courtesy, the enormous Genie faded away in a blaze of light and was gone.

Whereupon Mandricardo, having picked himself up,
dusted himself off, retrieved both sword and helm, and
having also and at length managed to pull that dashed
cloak of his off of his head so that he could see clearly
again, was staring sternly about him, saying, "Have at
you *now*, by my halidom! Where are you, sirrah?"

Ahd he simply could not understand why, at the
sight of him, Callipygia burst out laughing and sat down
on a conveniently placed boulder to have her laughter
out in relative comfort.

They rounded up the horses without any particular
difficulties and flew over the broad river by means of
the Magic Flying Carpet, but then dismounted, rolled
up the handy conveyance, and tucked it away among
the luggage which was packed on Minerva's broad and
capable back, for, as Mandricardo phrased it—

"I say, Cally, what, let's not Carpet to the capital,
but ride there. Like to see a bit of the countryside, you
know. Never been in Amazonia, meself. Dashed Carpet
gives one a spectacular view, I'd be the first to admit it,
what—but I *do* like just ridin' along, you know the
road or whatever."

So they proceeded by horseback from that point across
the green and fertile plains of Amazonia, and they had
not gone very far before they noticed a sizable body of
horsemen (well, to be precise, it was horse*women*,
this being Amazonia) who seemed to be approaching
them. When they got near enough for you to be able to
discern their features, Callipygia gave a *whoop!* and
the other riders also gave a *whoop!* and in no time to

speak of, everybody was out of the saddle and hugging and kissing each other, leaving Mandricardo alone still mounted and looking rather bewildered and saying "What, what?" to himself vaguely.

Then his lady-love turned and beckoned him and he dismounted and strode over to be introduced.

"Well, what do you think, dear? But these are all of my *sisters*, can you believe it?" said Callipygia, looking both happy and flustered all at the same time. "How fortuitous that you girls should come riding along at this time, I mean, really!"

And then she presented to her fiancé a bewildering succession of very pretty faces. There was a splendid tall girl with red hair and green eyes and freckles, rather boyish and hardly more than in her 'teens, who was named Antiope; and a very fair-skinned lass with shining black tresses and huge dark eyes, whom Callipygia addressed as Penthesileia; and a striking blonde girl with a lovely golden tan and clear blue eyes like twin sapphires, whose name was Hippolyta; and, well, there were sixteen of them in all, and I am not going to take up so much of your time as it would take to introduce them all to you.

I will remark on this, though, that from the bewildering differences among each of her sisters—for, really, when you examined it fairly, there were no two of them that looked anything much like one of the others—well, Sir Mandricardo rather got the impression (but was very much too polite to *ask*) that each of Callipygia's sisters had had a different father. This may or may not have been the case, but even Herodotus has little or nothing to say about the marriage customs of the Amazons, so I'm afraid that we must leave this interesting question unresolved.

Now the sixteen girls whispered and giggled amongst themselves, as sisters will do the world over, and stole little bright-eyes sidewise glances at the tall and stalwart Tartar knight, as he stood even taller than usual and sucked his tummy in and twirled his drooping black moustachios rather self-consciously, and it became at length more than obvious that, as far as they were concerned, Callipygia had certainly had good luck in her husband-hunting. . . .

"Oh, Callipygia," said Antiope, the teen-aged sister with the red hair, "just wait until Mother shows you her newest tapestry!"

"*And* the new curtains in the upstairs sitting-room," added Hippolyta.

"And did you know Hera—that's one of our cows, Sir Mandricardo; Cally virtually raised her from birth, you know—has *three* calves by now?" said Penthesileia.

And, all chattering away like so many magpies— thought Mandricardo, rather indulgently, bending a fond glance on his lady-love, who, pink and flustered and excited to be home again, was chattering away every bit as magpie-ish as any of them—they turned and began to wend their way across the verdant plain.

In the distance—as you followed the silvery and meandering course of the broad and shallow river Thermodon, wandering on its leisurely way to mingle its waters with those of the Euxine Sea which you could just barely glimpse, glinting pewter-like on the horizon— the rich shafts of the sun, which by now was westering, twinkled, flashed, and glittered in the thousand windows of Themiscyra, and gleamed from the burnished helms and the polished spearheads of the girl sentinels who stood here and there about the great wall of the city, and sparkled from the facets of the perfectly enormous red carbuncles and yellow topazes and blue alexandrines that were set into the greenish copper domes that lifted, together with a veritable forest of towers and turrets, from the purpling earth into the luminous and yet darkling skies which arched over Amazonia in particular and Pontus and these parts of the earth in general.

And, still chattering away a mile a minute with her sixteen sisters, Callipygia touched her spurs—but lightly—to the sides of her splendid roan mare, Blondel; and they picked up their pace just a little, for she thought that with a little bit of luck, they should come riding through the great granite gates into the courtyard of her mother's palace just in time for dinner. . . .

And there let us leave them for a while, riding through the late afternoon sunshine toward that pleasant and splendid goal.

EXPLICIT

The Notes
to Mandricardo

CHAPTER ONE

Mandricardo, son of King Agricane. This is not the same
Mandricardo, son of King Agricane of Tartary, who
fought against Roland and Oliver at Roncesvalles in
the *Song of Roland; that* Mandricardo was one of the
ancestors of *our* Mandricardo. Suffice it to say that,
such was his admiration for the heroes of chivalry,
had our Mandricardo been present in the Pyrenees
that famous day, he would have been fighting on
Roland's side along with the Twelve Peers. All of the
Tartarian kings bear the name of Agricane, you see,
and all of their firstborn sons are named Mandricardo.
Don't ask me why.

Trolls. We have it on the authority of the historian
Ibsen, in his admirable treatise *Peer Gynt*, that Trolls
fear Cold Steel; and Keightley, in *The Fairy Mythology*,
informs us that they distinctly dislike the sound of
church bells ringing. (I just thought I'd put that in; it
has nothing to do with our story.)

Bronze ring, inscription upon. An illustration in my
copy of the *Chronicle Narrative* displays the characters cut into the bronze ring; they are unquestionably
in the "Crossing the River" script, an alphabet used
only by magicians. You can find this alphabet in most
books on ceremonial magic, as it is no particular
secret.

CHAPTER TWO

Five Magicians. The history of the Five Magicians is, as I said, too long to be related here, and, also, it is too good a yarn to ruin with a mere synopsis. So you go and hunt it up yourself. You will find it in Frank R. Stockton's delightful little gem of a book *Ting-a-Ling Tales* (1882). The magicians are named Akbeck, Zamcar, Ormanduz, Mahalla, and Alcahazar. Alcahazar is the oldest of them.

Pyramids. The ancient Egyptians (who, after all, ought to know) called them by their names as given here, "Divine is Mycerinius," and so on. They were built by the rulers of the Old Kingdom (2780–2100 B.C.), and as their glistening limestone facings are long since stripped from them in the Lands We Know, it is pleasant to know they are still kept in decent repair in Terra Magica.

  The first pyramid was built by Khufu (whom the Greeks called Cheops), the first pharaoh of the IV Dynasty, the second by Khephren (Chephren), and the third by Menkaure (Mycerinius). The Greeks were always messing up everybody's name, calling Ramses "Rhampsinitus," for instance. I don't know just why. As for the Greek writers who dealt with the pyramids and their histories, we know of Aristogoras, Demoteles, Apion, Duris of Samos, Euhemerus, and Antisthenes. Unfortunately—for us as for them—all of their works are lost.

  Besides the "Big Three" of the Gizeh group, given above, there are many more pyramids of some size and distinction, like the four that stand in a row south of Gizeh, called the Abusir group, which were built by pharaohs of the V Dynasty. Incidentally, reluctant as I am to spoil a good juicy story, there is no truth to the old legend that the courtesan Rhodopis built the

little pyramid near Mycerinius' as her tomb, which
she financed out of her illicit earnings. That is pure
legend, as if the story that the mummy of King
Harmaïs is sepulchred in a secret burial chamber
somewhere inside the Sphinx. *That* tall-tale got into
Pliny, even; but Pliny was too hard-headed to swallow it.

I'm kind of sorry the Rhodopis story is just a myth;
she had quite a history (in her early days, before she
hit the big time, Rhodopis was a fellow-slave of the
philosopher—fabulist, really—Aesop).

I don't think anyone knows for sure whether or not
the pyramids of Gizeh had Guardian Idols like the
one I have described in this chapter, but even if they
did, I doubt if they were animated by magic to kill
or scare off burglars and other unwelcome visitors.
The story, as well as the description of this Idol of
black and white onyx, comes from an Arab writer
named Masoudi, who died about 967 AD; it was the
Islamic legend-mongers like Masoudi who are responsible for attributing the pyramids to Soliman
Djinn-Ben-Djinn and so on, and for the notion that
they were built before the Flood.

You can read all about this stuff in Leonard
Cottrell's admirable book, *The Mountains of Pharaoh*
(1956). Oh, incidentally, the names of the other pyra-
mids are like "Pure are the Places of Userkhaf,"
"Enduring is the Beauty of Pepi," "Beautiful are the
Places of Unis," and like that. Read Cottrell.

CHAPTER THREE

Mother Gothel. According to the Brothers Grimm, this
   was the name of the witch who locked Rapunzel up
   in that tower. As related to my novel *Kesrick*, she
   later obtained possession of Baba Yaga's hut on chicken

legs, and was melted by water like the Wicked Witch of the West in *The Wizard of Oz*.

Callipygia F. I am indebted to the historian Milne, in his *Once Upon a Time*, for instructing me in the manner in which princesses in magical countries sign their names. (The "F" stands for *Fecit*.)

"By Theseus' Toenails!" The Princess here gives voice to a typical Amazon curse, swearing, in fact, by one of her ancestors (or by a portion of his anatomy, at least), for Duke Theseus of Athens was wed to her ancestress, Hippolyta II, Queen of Amazonia. You can read all about their nuptials in a treatise called *A Midsummer Night's Dream*, by the historian Shakespeare.

"By Hercules' Hangnail!" Here Callipygia swears by the appendage of another ancestor, for the celebrated Hercules was, however briefly, wed to the Amazonian Queen Hippolyta I. (I don't know how many Hippolytas there were in all; these are the only two I have any information about.)

CHAPTER FOUR

Prince Camaralzaman. The proper nouns here are as given by the historian Lang in his excellent redaction of the tale, which you will find in his version of *The Arabian Nights Entertainments*. (See the story "Prince Camaralzaman and the Princess Badoura".)

"Fly, Carpet!" This is the correct and proper command to give a Magic Flying Carpet, as everyone knows who has ever seen Sabu use the same phrase in Sir Alexander Korda's admirable film, *The Thief of Bagdad* (1940). I am nothing if not scrupulous in my research.

CHAPTER FIVE

King Solomon. Whether or not this particular specimen
had once belonged to the famous King Solomon or
not, the *Chronicle Narrative* leaves uncertain; it was,
however, certainly not the same one which Prince
Houssain, the eldest of the three sons of the Sultan of
the Indies, bought in the marketplace of Bisnagar, as
related in "Prince Achmed and the Fairy Paribanou,"
in the *Arabian Nights*. That particular carpet, you
may recall, was among the christening gifts bestowed
by the fairies upon the infant Prigio, in *Prince Prigio*,
an historical work by the scholarly Mr. Lang: there is
no reason not to believe it still to be found among the
most treasured heirlooms of the Royal Family of
Pantouflia.

Pamphyllia. A country in Asia Minor, once a province
of the Roman Empire, and long since vanished from
the atlases of Terra Cognita, the Lands We Know.

The Enchanter Gorgonzola. This is not the Gorgonzola
who appears in Count de Caylus' story, "Heart of
Ice," which you will find in the *Green Fairy Book;*
That one was a fairy. No, this is the same enchanter
Gorgonzola later dispatched by King Prigio's son,
Prince Ricardo, as told in another work by the histo-
rian Lang called (rather appropriately) *Prince Ricardo*.
The historian Lang seems to crop up rather often in
these Notes, doesn't he?

CHAPTER SIX

"By Memnon's Moustache!" Again, Callipygia swears by
a portion of one of her ancestors; this one is Memnon,
King of Ethiopia and one of the heroes of the Trojan
War, who enjoyed a brief romance with the Amazonian
Queen, Penthesilea, during that celebrated unpleasant-

ness. You can read about it in an epic poem called *The Fall of Troy* by Quintus Smyrnaeus, rendered into English by Arthur S. Way and published in the Loeb classical Library.

My notebooks are loaded with this sort of stuff.

Florizel. "Florizel" is an old family name of the royalty of seacoast Bohemia, and it does seem a trifle surprising to find it here in Lower Pamphyllia. The answer is simply that King Rumberto married a Bohemian princess who named her son after several ancestors; Rumberto didn't much care, since all princes get eight or ten first names when they are christened anyway. (His *full* name was Florizel Sigismundo Waldemar Gustavus Ferdinandus Lorenzo Dagobert Ignazio von Hohenzollern.)

CHAPTER SEVEN

Mahoum, Golfarin, etc. The historian Rabelais informs us, in his *Gargantua and Pantagruel,* that suchlike Paynims as Moors and Saracens and similar riff-raff swear by these Idols. Sir John de Mandeville is my authority for the last, Termagant.

Salamandre. It was the learned Paracelsus who provided each of the four elements with its respective genius: Fire (the Salamandres), Water (the Undinas), Air (the Sylphs), and Earth (the Gnomes). He unfortunately neglected to provide the same service for the fifth Classical element, Aether.

Celebrated painter. It must have been the same Tomaso Lorenzo whose skills at portraiture are praised so highly in the historian Thackeray's distinguished treatise, *The Rose and the Ring.*

CHAPTER NINE

Barodo-Euralian War. You can read all about this nota-
ble conflict in *Euralia Past and Present*, Chapters
IX-XII by the former Euralian court historian, Roger
Scurvilegs. Since copies of that work are more easily
come by in Terra Magica than in the Lands We
Know, I recommend A. A. Milne's *Once Upon a
Time* for a charming version of the same material.

CHAPTER TEN

Articiocchi. The author of the book to which Florizel
refers is obviously a member of the distinguished
Articiocchi family of Crim Tartary, mentioned by the
historian Thackeray in his treatise *The Rose and the
Ring*, elsewhere cited in these Notes. No doubt an
artichoke was featured prominently on the coat-of-
arms of this noble family. (Crim Tartary is nowhere
near Tartary proper, by the way; it is the same thing
as the Crimea in Russia.)
Dictionary of Famous Quests. Known only in the librar-
ies of Terra Magica, I'm sorry to say. And what a
pity: now *there's* a book I'd dearly love to read.
Signore Spinacchi. I'll bet I can guess what's on the
coat-of-arms of *his* family, too!

CHAPTER ELEVEN

Mahoum, Golfarin, Termagant. As noted elsewhere
above, these are Idols before whom, in their despicable ignorance, grovel the heathenish Paynims. The
names appear variously in the works of the historian
Rabelais and the geographer de Mandeville.
Brumagem. Another Idol worshiped by the vile Paynims, but one hitherto unmentioned by Western writ-

ers. My own contribution to the pantheon of Paynimry, if you like.

Chapter Thirteen

Remora and Firedrake. Those interested in this famous quest are advised to consult the book *Prince Prigio*, a work by the historian Lang, as you should know by this time. References to the famous combat may also be found in two subsequent volumes of Pantouflian history, *Prince Ricardo* and *Tales of a Fairy Court* by the same author. They will well repay your labor in searching for copies of them. "Jolly good stuff," as Mandricardo would say.

Chapter Fourteen

By the Deggial. The Wicked Enchanter here swears a fearful oath, taking in vain the dreaded name of the Mussulmans' "Anti-christ." Only a black-hearted Paynim would dare use such an oath, of course.

Cabalflorus DG., etc. A gold coin of this description is mentioned in *The Rose and the Ring*, a treatise by the historian Thackeray to which I have earlier alluded. It was obviously minted in Crim Tartary during the reign of the Emperor Cavolfiore. Those desirous of further information are directed to the consultation of that completely admirable historical work.

Chapter Fifteen

King of Rubazania. For more information on this monarch and a visit to his Court, see my fantasy novel for children, *Quite a Carpet!*; that is, you can see it if I can ever find a publisher who wishes to print the thing.

King Alphonso of Puffleburg. A small country near
Pantouflia, Puffleburg is just north of Orn. You
may visit it in my book *Summer Magic*, if, like
the novel mentioned above, it ever finds a publisher.
(*sigh*)

Order of the Radish, etc. Frankly, I don't have the
slightest idea why the rulers of magical kingdoms
name their knightly orders after vegetables, but they
do, in point of fact. See *Prince Prigio*, *Prince Ricardo*, *The Rose and the Ring* and *Petsetilla's Posy*,
by Tom Hood, if you don't believe me. I am just
continuing the grand and glorious tradition.

CHAPTER SIXTEEN

Akhdar. As noted in the text of this redaction, this
Akhdar belonged to the Marids, a powerful and nu-
merous nation of the Genii. What the text of the
Chronicle Narrative does not point out, however, is
that this Akhdar is the brother of a dangerous Efreet
called Azrag the Blue, who made an appearance of
his own quite early in these histories, in which he
was tricked and foiled by Kesrick and Arimaspia and
the sorcerer Pteron, who had invaded his enchanted
palace atop a peak in the Rhiphaean Mountains.

Smaragdines. These are a kind of old-fashioned emerald.

By Zaqqum and the Zamzam. These are the sort of
things by which wicked Paynims curse; if you don't
believe me, just consult the notes to the Burton
Society edition of the *Arabian Nights*.

CHAPTER SEVENTEEN

Enormous Cavern. The description here of the Caverns
of Akhdar are so close in their detail to descriptions
of the Hall of Eblis in Beckford's *Vathek* that I am

inclined to the suspicion that Akhdar designed his manse in emulation of that of Eblis.

Aptly named. That is, the Arabic word for the color green is *akhdar*. This alone would tend to suggest, did I not already know it to be the truth, that Akhdar was the brother of Azraq the Blue, since these jokes run in families and *azraq* means "blue."

Getiafrose. Akhdar here swears by the all-powerful Queen of the Genii.

Shadukiam. The capital city of the empire of the Genii, famed for its rosy domes.

CHAPTER EIGHTEEN

Aphania. Something of the history of this kingdom, and all about how Princess Petsetilla was wooed and won by Count Remsky, can be found in a book called *Petsetilla's Posy*, by Thomas Hood. Yes, the poet. I say "can be found," perhaps I should say "may be found," for you will probably have a bit of trouble finding the book, since it was published in 1870.

Battle of Rimbombamento. For this famous conflict, see the historian Thackeray's distinguished treatise, *The Rose and the Ring*.

By Kashkash. The Marid here swears by the very oldest of all the Genii. See Sir Richard Francis Burton's notes to the *Arabian Nights*.

CHAPTER NINETEEN

By Loki's lower lip. Mandricardo here swears by the Devils of such mythologies as the Norse, Zoroastrian and Babylonish.

Bleps, Strycophanes, et al. It is no doubt purely accidental, but these just happen to be five of the eight fabulous monsters which Florian de Puysange encountered in the ill-rumored Wood of Acaire, in James Branch Cabell's excellent fantasy novel, *The High Place*. In that novel, they guarded the only approach to the castle of Brunbelois.

Fons Iuventutem. The notes to the *Chronicle Narrative* at this point remark that Mandricardo and Callipygia had found their way to the elusive country of Cockaigne, a wondrous magical land wherein may be found everything that is best in life. That Fons Juventutem, the Fountain of Youth, is situated in Cockaigne is a datum found nowhere else than in the *Chronicle Narrative*, but it makes excellent sense. After all, youth is one of the best things in life, as my reader will have excellent cause to realize once he no longer has it.

CHAPTER TWENTY

Tarandus. The animal is as it is here described, chameleonlike qualities and all. It was another of the fabulous beasts encountered by Florian in the wood of Acaire in *The High Place*, where it was called the only one of its kind.

Them. Whatever Gods or Powers or Authorities established the Old Man in his position are left unnamed in the *Chronicle Narrative*, and I shall follow the excellent example of that book, although I suspect the Léshy had a hand in it.

Syl and Soham. Two more legendary creatures, these from Islamic folklore, and both appearing in Beckford's immortal *Vathek*. You really should read *Vathek*, you know.

CHAPTER TENTY-ONE

Apsu, Set, Vukub-Kakix. Mandricardo here swears by
   various anatomical parts of the Devils of the Assyrian,
   Egyptian and Quiche Maya mythologies. (For the
   Quiche Maya, see the *Popul Voh.*)

CHAPTER TWENTY-TWO

The Leshy. The Leshy are Russian wood-fays. Outside
   of their frequent appearance in Russian folklore and
   fairy-tales, they are principally known to us from the
   novels of James Branch Cabell. In the Cabellian cos-
   mos they are more-than-mortal beings of great power,
   more or less in charge of the world, under, of course,
   Higher Authority.
Including, as of right now, Cockaigne. Unlike most of
   the countries of which Terra Magica is comprised,
   Cockaigne has no fixed and permanent location, but
   moves about as it wills. (You will notice that I cautiously said unlike "most" of the countries in Terra
   Magica; I do not count, of course, the Land of Green
   Ginger.)
Catoblepas. You will find him in your bestiary: he is
   notable for having a long and flabby and very weak
   neck, so weak that he cannot manage to lift his head
   off the ground.
Flock or Pack. The confusion over the proper collective
   noun is due to the fact that Senmurvs are dog-headed
   eagles found in Persian folklore.

CHAPTER TWENTY-THREE

Themiscyra on the Thermodon, etc. It was the historian Herodotus who informed us that the country of
   the Amazons occupied the former regions of Pontus,

fronting upon the Euxine Sea, and that the capital of this nation, called Themiscyra, was situated upon the shores of the river Thermodon. See the *Histories*, or any competent Classical dictionary.

Ithuriel. According to Voltaire, in his excellent brief treatise, "The World as it Goes," the great and puissant Ithuriel, a powerful Prince of the Genii, is in charge of Persia and its environs. You can find this invaluable treatise in my Doubleday anthology, *Kingdoms of Sorcery*, under the title of "The History of Babouc the Scythian."

CHAPTER TWENTY-FOUR

Antiope, etc. It would seem that some of the seventeen daughters of Queen Megamastaia are named after their famous ancestresses: Antiope was an Amazonian princess with whom the hero Theseus had a brief fling; Penthesileia was a Queen of the Amazons who fought in the Trojan War on the losing side, and was slain in battle by the redoubtable Achilles (in the *Posthomerica* of Quintus Smyrnaeus, a Greek epic which tells what happened *post homerica*, "after Homer," that is. It's a sequel to the *Iliad*; and it was from Hippolyta, the Amazonian Queen, that Hercules thieved the famous magical girdle.

My notebooks are loaded with this sort of useless but interesting information . . . hope you've enjoyed it!

The End of the Notes
to *Mandricardo*

DAW

DAW Presents
Magic and Sorcery and Wondrous Adventures

B.W. Clough
The Averidan Novels

In the realm of Averidan nothing works out the way it's planned, especially under the reign of the Crystal Crown. From wizards' wars to barbarian invasions ... from a farmer made king in spite of himself to a journey into the mysterious realms of magical power, here is a spellbinding new fantasy series where high enchantment rules supreme.

☐ THE DRAGON OF MISHBIL   (UE2078—$2.95)
☐ THE CRYSTAL CROWN   (UE1922—$2.75)
☐ THE REALM BENEATH   (UE2137—$2.95)

Marion Zimmer Bradley
The Sword and Sorceress Series

Marion Zimmer Bradley has assembled these treasures of heroic fantasy wherein women of courage and wizardry challenge the evils and dreads of a bewitched world. Here are new stories of warrior women and mistresses of magic by such authors as C.J. Cherryh, Glen Cook, Phyllis Ann Karr, Diana Paxson, Jennifer Roberson, Charles Saunders, and many more.

☐ SWORD AND SORCERESS I   (UE1928—$2.95)
☐ SWORD AND SORCERESS II   (UE2041—$2.95)
☐ SWORD AND SORCERESS III   (UE2141—$3.50)